Laine was there by [...] **him, and Tucker wasn't** [...] **the first move or even how it happened, but she ended up in his arms.**

Strange that it kept happening, and it shouldn't. Even a hug of comfort was a Texas-sized reminder that it was Laine in his arms and that nothing good could come of this.

Well, nothing reasonable anyway.

Maybe it was because every inch of him was on edge that he even thought of holding her as a stress reliever. Yeah, for a second or two, it was relief, but what always followed were some crystal clear reminders of why they shouldn't be doing this in the first place.

The heat between them.

The bad blood, too. Hard to hang on to bad blood, though, when the blasted attraction kept getting in the way.

COWBOY BEHIND THE BADGE

USA TODAY Bestselling Author
DELORES FOSSEN

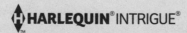 HARLEQUIN® INTRIGUE®

Recycling programs for this product may not exist in your area.

ISBN-13: 978-0-373-69788-5

COWBOY BEHIND THE BADGE

Printed in U.S.A.

ABOUT THE AUTHOR

USA TODAY bestselling author Delores Fossen has sold over fifty novels with millions of copies of her books in print worldwide. She's received the Booksellers' Best Award and the RT Reviewers' Choice Award, and was a finalist for a prestigious RITA® Award. In addition, she's had nearly a hundred short stories and articles published in national magazines. You can contact the author through her webpage at www.dfossen.net.

Books by Delores Fossen

HARLEQUIN INTRIGUE

CAST OF CHARACTERS

Texas Ranger Tucker McKinnon—The bad boy lawman of the McKinnon family. He's not daddy material, or so he thinks, until he's forced to protect two newborns and the woman he's long considered his enemy.

Laine Braddock—A child psychologist. She'll do anything to protect the babies she's rescued, even if it means turning to Tucker, the last man on earth who'd want to help her.

The newborns—They're too young to realize the danger or the people willing to risk their lives to keep them safe.

Dawn Cowen—A missing woman at the center of a black market baby farm investigation.

Martin Hague—A social worker who seems too eager to take the rescued babies from Tucker and Laine.

Darren Carty—Laine's ex-fiancé, who might have a personal stake in not just the investigation but in the babies that Laine rescued.

Rhonda Wesson—Once a victim of a notorious black market baby farm, but does she know more than she's saying?

Chapter One

Tucker McKinnon heard the sound the moment he stepped from the shower. Someone was moving around in his kitchen.

He opened his mouth to call out to his brothers, the only two people who would have let themselves into his house, but then he remembered. His older brother, Cooper, was on his honeymoon, and his kid brother, Colt, was working at the sheriff's office in town.

So, who was his visitor?

He didn't like most of the possibilities that came to mind. Heck, it could even be someone connected to the arrest he'd made just hours earlier. The dirt-for-brains fugitive that Tucker had tangled with could have sent someone out to settle the score with the Texas Ranger who'd hauled his sorry butt off to jail.

If so, the score-settler wasn't being very quiet, and had clearly lost the element of surprise.

Tucker dried off, wincing when he wiped the towel over the cuts and bruises. He wasn't that old, just thirty-four, but he was too old to be getting into a fistfight with the fugitive who'd gotten the jump on him.

Hurrying, Tucker pulled on his jeans and eased open the door so he could peek inside his bedroom. No one was there, so he grabbed his gun from the holster he'd ditched on the nightstand and stepped into the hall.

The sounds continued.

Someone mumbling. Other sounds, too. He heard the click of the lock on the back door. His intruder, whoever it was, had locked them in together.

Probably not a good sign.

Since he was barefoot, his steps didn't make any noise on the hardwood floors, and with his gun ready, Tucker inched down the short hall, past the living room, so he could look into the kitchen.

There was still plenty of light outside, but the trees next to his kitchen window made the room pretty dark and filled it with shadows. None of the shadows, however, looked like an intruder.

He saw the pantry door slightly ajar. A door Tucker was darn certain he'd shut because he was always stubbing his toe on it.

Someone was in there.

He glanced out the window. No vehicle other than his own truck. The sky looked like a crime scene, though. Bruise-colored storm clouds with a bloodred sunset stabbing through them. He hoped that wasn't some kind of bad sign.

"Not very bright," Tucker tossed out there. "Breaking into the house of a Texas Ranger. We tend to frown on stuff like that." He slapped on the lights.

"No," someone said. It was a woman, and even though her voice was only a whisper, there was as much emotion in it as if she'd shouted the word. "Turn off that light. I don't want them to see us."

"Them?" Tucker questioned.

"The killers."

Okay. That got his attention in more ways than one. Despite the whisper, he recognized the voice. "Laine?"

As in Laine Braddock, a child psychologist who sometimes worked with the Rangers and the FBI. Since they weren't on good terms—not on speaking terms, in fact— Tucker had worked with her as little as possible. After all, his mother, Jewell, had been charged with murdering Laine's father. That didn't create a warm, fuzzy bond between them.

Not now, anyway.

Once, when they were kids, Laine and he had played together almost every day. And she'd been on the receiving end of his very first kiss.

That wasn't exactly something he wanted to remember at this moment, though.

Tucker went closer to the door, and despite the fact he knew her, he didn't lower his gun. Everything inside his severely banged up body was yelling for him to stay alert so he wouldn't be on the receiving end of another butt-whipping. Especially since Laine might not be alone.

"What killers?" he asked.

"The ones who could have followed us here."

Tucker didn't miss the *us*.

There was no *us* when it came to Laine and him. Except they had run into each other about a week before, when he was called to assist the FBI with investigating a black-market adoption ring. Laine had been there on standby in case any of the children were recovered, but Tucker and she hadn't exchanged anything other than some frosty glares.

And that told him loads.

Even if so-called killers were involved, he was the

absolute last person on God's green earth that Laine would have come to, and yet here she was.

"How'd you get in?" he demanded.

"Through the back door. It wasn't locked."

Not locking up was a bad habit that Tucker would remedy the moment he got her out of there. "So you let yourself in. Not a smart thing to do, since you knew I'd be armed."

"It was a risk I had to take," she mumbled.

That only added to the whole puzzling situation. Why come here? What risk was worth a visit with the enemy?

Maybe she hadn't come here by choice.

"Come out so I can see you," Tucker ordered, because he wanted to make sure that someone wasn't holding a gun on her. Maybe it was those killers she'd warned him about.

"Turn out the lights first, please. I don't want them to see us."

Her presence, combined with the fear in her voice, was enough to make Tucker do as she said. He turned off the light, let his eyes adjust to the darkness and moved closer in case he had to fight off someone holding her hostage.

The hinges on the pantry door creaked a little when she fully opened it, and she stepped into the doorway. Yeah, it was Laine all right, and even in the dim light, Tucker could see that something was wrong. Everything about her was disheveled, from her brown hair to her clothes. There was mud or something on her jeans, shoes and white top.

She made a slight gasping sound and reached out to touch him, but then she jerked back her hand. "You've been hurt. Did they come here already?"

"No one's been here. I got this while making an arrest."

He must have looked downright awful for her to notice something like that at a time like this. "How'd you get out here? Where's your car? And why would someone have come here *already?*"

Laine pressed her hand to her head as if he'd just doled out too many questions. Heck, he was just getting started.

"I parked in the woods by the road and walked through the pasture to get here," she finally said. "I didn't want them following me, but they could come here looking for me."

Her voice was shaking. So was she. And she latched her hands onto the doorjamb as if that were the only way she could keep on her feet.

That unsteadiness sent a new round of concern through him. "Are you hurt? Do you need a doctor?"

"I wasn't hurt."

She swallowed hard, pushed herself from the doorway and came toward him. Despite the fact he still had a gun pointed at her. She landed in his arms before Tucker could stop her, and she started to cry. Not just any old crying, either. Sobs punctuated with hard breaths that made a hiccupping sound.

Oh, man.

Whatever this was, it was *really* bad.

Tucker would've needed a heart of ice not to react. And he reacted, all right. He slid his left arm around her. He kept his grip loose. Very loose. But it didn't matter. Basically, Laine was plastered against him, and he wasn't wearing a shirt. He could feel pretty much every inch of her trembling body.

"They killed her right in front of me," Laine said through the sobs.

That pushed aside anything he was feeling from the unexpected hugging session. "Who was killed?"

"A woman. I don't know her name."

Tucker eased back, met her gaze. "Start from the beginning. What happened?"

And then he'd want to know why she hadn't taken this to the local cops. After all, his brother was the sheriff, and his brother, Colt, the deputy. Yet, Laine had come all the way there to his family's ranch, which wasn't exactly on the beaten path.

"Remember that undercover assignment I was on last week?" She didn't wait for him to answer. "We were working on it together, but you got me fired."

Yeah, he remembered. "Not fired. I just asked for you to be reassigned somewhere not near me."

"You got me fired," she repeated, sounding not too happy about it. "Anyway, about an hour and a half ago, I got a call from a woman who wouldn't tell me who she was. She said she'd been held captive by guards at the place we were investigating. But she escaped today."

Laine stopped, shuddering, and pressed her fingers to her mouth.

Good grief. He hoped this wasn't going where he thought it was. "Please tell me you didn't go out to meet this woman alone?"

"I didn't have to go anywhere to meet her. She was in the parking lot outside my office in town. Hiding behind my car. She said she was making the call from a prepaid cell phone that she had stolen from her captors."

Tucker groaned and hoped the rest of this conversation would go a whole lot better than what he'd heard so far. "And at that point, you should have called my brother.

Colt's been on duty all day, and he would have responded immediately."

Laine didn't argue with that, even though Tucker was dead certain she didn't trust Colt any more than she trusted him or the rest of his family.

"The woman said not to contact the cops, that I had to see her alone. So I went out to the parking lot," Laine continued.

But she stopped, and the tears returned. Worse, her hands twitched as if she might reach for him again. She didn't, thank goodness. Instead, Laine held on to the counter by the sink.

"What happened?" Tucker pressed. He hated to sound impatient and insensitive, but if a murder had truly taken place, he needed to report it.

"The woman was scared. Terrified," Laine corrected. "And she only had a chance to say a few words to me when a car came screeching into the parking lot. She told me to run and hide. So I did. She said I was to stay in hiding, no matter what happened. I ducked behind the Dumpster."

Tucker knew that parking lot and the position of the Dumpster. Laine's office was on the far edge of Sweetwater Springs, in a small cottage that shared a back parking lot with three other small buildings. Two were empty, and the third was a law office. Tucker hoped someone else was in that office to witness what'd gone on, in case this turned into an investigation.

"If I'd known what was going to happen," Laine continued, "I wouldn't have hidden. I would have tried to get help." She pulled in a long breath, and the trembling got worse. "The car came to a stop, and two men jumped out. They were wearing police uniforms."

That gave him a moment's pause. "What kind?" The cops in Sweetwater Springs didn't often wear uniforms, but when they did, they were khaki-colored.

She shook her head. "I'm not sure. They were blue, and they had badges and guns."

Maybe they had been from another town or jurisdiction and they'd tracked the woman to Laine's office. "Did they try to arrest the woman?"

A sob tore from her throat. "No. She motioned for me to stay put and she ran. She bolted toward the street, and they shot her. Oh, God. Tucker, they shot her."

It didn't matter that he was a lawman. Hearing about a shooting hit him hard. Except something about this wasn't adding up. "Why didn't anyone report the shots? Why didn't *you* report them?"

"They used guns with silencers." She pressed her fingers to her mouth a moment. "They shot her in the back as she was running. She was dead. I could tell by how limp her arms and legs were when they picked up her body and threw her in the trunk of their car."

Hell.

Since it hadn't started raining yet, there'd be blood. Maybe even some other evidence.

Tucker's cell phone was in the bedroom by his holster, and he didn't want to leave the room to go get it. Instead, he reached for the landline on the kitchen wall. He had to call Colt and get him to the scene ASAP.

"Don't." Laine latched onto his wrist. "They had a police radio in their car. I heard it. And if you call the sheriff's office, they'll hear it, too. They'll know I came here."

Tucker blew out a long, frustrated breath. Not good about the police radio, but like uniforms, they could be faked or stolen. It didn't mean cops had actually killed the woman.

"Why *did* you come here?" he asked.

Laine let that question hum between them for several moments. "Because I knew the lawman in you would help me."

Tucker let her answer hum between them a couple of moments, too, even though he couldn't argue with it since it was the truth. "The murder has to be reported, but I'll tell my brother not to put any of this on the police radio. Did you get the license plate on the car?"

"No. Sorry. I wasn't thinking straight." Another sob. "I should have done something to stop them."

"If you'd tried, they likely would have killed you, too." It was the truth, and even though Laine and he were essentially enemies, he didn't wish that on anybody. As it was, this nightmare would be with her for a long time.

He reached for the phone again, but once more Laine stopped him. "I stayed hidden like the woman told me to do. I did everything she insisted that I do." Her voice was frantic now, and she sounded like she was on the verge of a full-blown panic attack. "And the words she said to me keep repeating in my head."

Everything inside Tucker went still. "What words?"

"'Hide them. Protect them.'" She turned, maybe to bolt out the door, so he took her by the shoulders.

"Who's *them?*" He groaned. Were there more women still being held at the baby farm? That wouldn't be good, because if everything Laine had told him was true, their captors were cold-blooded killers.

She pried off his grip and went back to the door of the pantry.

Tucker braced himself to see his pantry crammed with

women who were on the run from the men who'd gunned down one of their fellow captives.

But there were no women.

In fact, because the lights were off, Tucker couldn't see anything other than the food on the shelves.

"I have to protect them," Laine repeated, her voice breaking.

Tucker went closer to the pantry and looked around. On the floor was a rumpled blanket.

Except it wasn't just a blanket.

Wrapped in the center of it was something he'd never expected to find in his pantry.

Two sleeping newborn babies.

Chapter Two

Laine tried to brace herself for Tucker's reaction. By all accounts, he was a good lawman, so she doubted that he would just toss the babies and her out the door. It was one of the reasons she'd come to him. That, and there being literally no one else she could trust.

She wasn't sure she could trust him, either.

But she was certain that he'd do what was right for the babies.

"They need to be protected," Laine said when Tucker just stood there volleying glances between her and the babies. "The killers will be looking for them. And for me."

Tucker shook his head, obviously trying to process this. She wished him luck with that. She'd had more than an hour to process it, and it still didn't make sense.

"Why are you so sure the killers will be looking for you?" he snapped.

"Because if they don't know already, they'll find out I'm the person renting that office space, that it was my car the woman was hiding behind. And that I had a connection to the illegal adoption investigation."

He made a sound of agreement with frustration mixed

in. He tore his gaze from the babies. "How'd this woman know to come to you?"

"I'm not sure. She didn't get a chance to tell me." In fact, the only thing Laine was certain of was the woman's warning that kept repeating through her head.

Hide them. Protect them.

"I don't know anything about these particular babies," Laine said. The panic started to crawl through her again. "But I'm sure they'll be hungry soon. I figured since you have a nephew, you might be able to get some baby supplies."

What Tucker did do was curse and reach for the phone again. Once again, she tried to stop him, but before he could make a call she didn't want him to make, the phone rang. The sound shot through the room and sent her heart slamming against her chest. It also caused the babies to stir.

"Colt," Tucker said when he answered. Someone that she knew well. Colt was his kid brother and the deputy sheriff of Sweetwater Springs. He was also someone else she wasn't sure she could trust. "I was just about to call you."

Tucker still had his gun gripped in his hand, and he turned his steely-gray lawman's eyes to the window when he put the call on speaker.

"I tried your cell phone first and when I didn't get an answer, I called the landline. Good thing you're there. Just had an interesting visit from two San Antonio cops looking for Laine Braddock," Colt continued. "They said they had a warrant for her arrest."

Oh, mercy. It was a lie, of course. There was no warrant out on her, but this had to be the two men who'd killed the woman.

"Are they still there?" Laine blurted out. "If so, arrest them."

"Laine?" Colt mumbled. He said her name like profanity. "Tucker, what the hell's she doing at your place?"

"I'm trying to figure that out now. Why'd the men want to arrest her?"

"Aiding and abetting an escaped felon." Colt paused. "Did she?"

"No!" Laine insisted.

At the same moment, Tucker said, "I'm trying to figure that out, too. Was there anything suspicious about these men?"

"Nothing that I noticed. Why?"

"Just check and make sure they're really cops. I have an old friend in SAPD, Lieutenant Nate Ryland. Call him and make sure these two guys are from his department. Another thing I need you to do is get someone out to Laine's office ASAP and check the back parking lot for any signs of an attack."

"An attack? What the devil's going on?" Colt pressed.

"Just send someone over there and let me know if there's anything to find."

"And don't use your police radio," Laine insisted. "The men are probably monitoring the airwaves, and they might try to go back and clean up before you can investigate the scene."

Colt, no doubt, wanted to ask plenty more questions, but Tucker cut him off. "I'll be in touch after I've made some more calls." With that, Tucker hung up and headed out of the room and into the hall.

"What calls?" Laine asked, following him. She couldn't go far in case the babies started to cry, but thankfully the hall wasn't that long.

Tucker ducked into a room—his bedroom, she soon realized. He grabbed a black T-shirt that'd been draped over a chair. He slipped it on.

No more bare chest.

And she hated that she'd even noticed something like that at a time like this. Of course, it was hard not to notice a man who looked like Tucker McKinnon. That rumpled sandy-brown hair. Those eyes.

That amazing body.

Laine was counting heavily on him using that lawman's body if it came down to protecting the babies.

He looked up at her as he tugged on his boots, and his left eyebrow slid up. Only then did Laine realize that she was gawking at him.

"What calls?" she repeated. Obviously, the murder she'd witnessed had caused her brain to turn cloudy.

"Social services, for one. We have to turn these babies over to the proper authorities."

"What if these killers have connections there, too?" She didn't wait for him to answer. "It's too risky to call anyone now. We need to find someone we can trust before we let anyone know we have the babies."

Tucker gave her a flat look, as if she'd lost her mind. Heck, maybe she had.

"Look, you've been through a bad experience," he said, his tone not exactly placating, but close enough. "And because someone else broke the law, that doesn't mean we have the right to do the same. The babies need to be turned over to social services so they can find out who they are. It's possible the woman who was hiding behind the car isn't even their mother."

That hit her like an avalanche. Because it might be true. God, why hadn't she thought of that? Except she remembered the look of desperation on the woman's face. Her plea for help.

Hide them. Protect them.

And Laine had to shake her head. "She sacrificed her life for them. Only their mother would have done that. A kidnapper would have just handed them over to the killers to save herself."

Tucker stared at her. And stared. Before he mumbled some profanity and snatched up his phone from the nightstand. "A friend of a friend is married to a social worker. I'll arrange a meeting with her."

A meeting like that still wasn't without risks, but it was better than involving the cops. Of course, if Colt found blood or something else in the parking lot, Laine seriously doubted that he would keep the information to himself.

At some point, all of this had to become official.

Laine heard a soft, kittenlike sound and hurried back to the pantry. One of the babies was stirring. The other was still sound asleep. Laine went closer, knelt beside them and tried to gently rock the baby with her hand.

"My friend didn't answer," Tucker said, coming back into the kitchen. "So I left a message." He tipped his head to the babies. "Are they boys or girls?"

"I don't know." She'd been so focused on getting them to safety that she hadn't considered anything else. But Laine considered it now.

Both babies wore full-length body gowns with drawstrings at the bottoms. She loosened the one on the squirming baby and peeked inside the diaper.

"This one's a boy," she relayed to Tucker. She had a look at the other one. "And this one's a girl."

The different sexes could mean they weren't twins after all, though they looked alike and appeared to be the same age. But what if the dead woman had rescued her own child and then someone else's? It could mean there was another woman being held captive.

Or another woman who was already dead.

That sickened Laine even more.

"If my friend doesn't call back in the next few minutes, we'll need to get someone else out here to take them," Tucker explained. "I mean, we don't even have any way to feed them. My nephew's two, and he doesn't drink from a bottle. I doubt we'd even have anything like that around the ranch."

Laine couldn't dispute what he was saying. Nor could she push aside the feeling that these babies felt like her responsibility now.

Tucker mumbled something she didn't catch and went to the kitchen window to look out again. When the baby kept squirming and started to fuss, Laine eased him into her arms.

She had little experience holding a baby, and even though she'd run through the pasture with them, the babies had been wrapped in that bulky blanket. With nothing but the gown and his diaper between them, the baby felt as fragile as paper-thin crystal.

Tucker glanced at her and frowned. "You know what you're doing?"

"No." But the baby did seem to settle down when she rocked him, so Laine kept doing it. "I'm sorry for bringing them to your doorstep, but I drove out of town as fast as I could and didn't know where else to go."

She glanced around the kitchen. "We used to play here when we were kids."

"Yeah. It was my grandfather's house."

The explanation was clipped, as if it were the last thing

he wanted to discuss with her. Maybe because they'd done more than just play in this house. They'd shared a childhood kiss there. She had been ten. Tucker, eleven. Twenty-three years ago.

Just days before her father's murder.

After that, there'd been no kissing.

No more playing together. No more friendship.

Even though she'd just been a kid, it hadn't taken long before Laine had realized what gossip everyone was spreading—that Tucker's mother, Jewell, and her father, Whitt, had done something bad. Later, she would come to understand that *something bad* meant they'd been lovers. And that Jewell had murdered her father when he'd tried to break things off and work on saving his marriage. A murder that Jewell had yet to be punished for. At least now the woman was in jail, awaiting trial.

"Don't," Tucker warned, as if he knew exactly what she was thinking. "I don't want to take any trips down memory lane right now."

Fair enough. His mother was a touchy subject for both of them. From everything Laine had heard, Tucker and his brothers weren't disputing Jewell's guilt. They only wanted the woman who'd cheated on their father and abandoned them to get out of their lives and leave Sweetwater Springs.

Tucker's cell phone rang, causing the baby to fuss again, and Laine leaned in so she could see the caller's name on the screen.

Colt.

The fear returned with a vengeance, and she prayed that Tucker's brother had found something—anything— that would help her keep the babies safe.

Laine leaned in so she'd be able to hear what he said.

Obviously she leaned too close, because her arm brushed against Tucker's chest. He shot her a "back off" scowl and hit the speaker function so she'd be able to hear.

"Just got off the phone with Lieutenant Ryland," Colt immediately said. "He doesn't know a thing about two SAPD cops coming to Sweetwater Springs."

"So they're fake," Laine concluded.

"Looks that way. And there's also no warrant for your arrest."

She hadn't expected to feel as much relief as she did. Laine knew she'd done nothing to have an arrest warrant issued against her, and the last thing she needed right now was real cops trying to arrest her for a fake warrant.

"What about the parking lot?" Tucker asked. "You find anything?"

"I sent Reed to check it out. Still waiting to hear from him."

He was talking about Reed Caldwell, one of the deputies. Laine hoped the two men who'd fired those shots had managed to leave some kind of evidence behind. And then she thought of something else.

"Maybe the dead woman's fingerprints are somewhere on my car? She had her hand on the door when I first spotted her."

"Dead woman?" Colt questioned.

Tucker groaned and rubbed his hand over his face. "Laine thinks she witnessed a murder."

"I don't *think* it. I *know* I did."

"She witnessed a shooting," Tucker said, "by two men dressed as cops. Her car's parked in the woods near my place. When Reed's done with the parking lot, can you send him out to check for prints?"

"Sure. But you know as well as I do, if there was really

a murder, I need Laine down here now to make an official report."

Tucker glanced at her and then at the baby she was holding. "There's a complication. The woman left two babies, and they're newborns by the looks of it. Any reports of missing babies?"

"None," Colt said without hesitation. "If something like that had come in, I would have known."

Yes, he probably would. Amber Alerts got top priority, even in a small-town sheriff's office.

"But I'll make some calls," Colt continued. "Maybe this is a case of parental abduction and the local authorities haven't reported it yet."

Tucker mumbled his thanks. "Hold on a second, Colt." He motioned toward Laine's phone. "Give it to me."

It took some doing, balancing the baby while working her way into her jeans pocket to retrieve the phone. She handed it to Tucker.

Normally, Laine wouldn't have been wearing jeans on a workday, but she hadn't had any appointments. She'd simply gone in to catch up on paperwork and rearrange some things in her office.

As bad as her situation was, she shuddered to think of how much worse it could have been if she hadn't been there to rescue the babies. Either the killers would have found them, or else it would have been heaven knows how long before someone spotted them in the parking lot.

Tucker scrolled through the list of calls she'd received and read Colt the number of the last one on the list. It was the one from the woman.

"It's possible that phone was stolen from those two fake cops," Tucker explained to his brother. "It's also possible that it's a prepaid cell."

It was clear with his *possible* comments that Tucker was withholding judgment about the veracity of her story. But every word of it was true.

Colt didn't respond to that right away, but she heard some movement on the other end of the line. "Yeah, it's a burner all right, and it's no longer in service."

Laine tried not to groan because it might disturb the baby, but it was hard to hold back her disappointment. That phone number could have given them clues about the men's identities.

The dead woman's, too.

"Call me if Reed finds anything in the parking lot," Tucker added. He ended the call and turned to her. "I can't sit on this any longer. If that woman was murdered, then every minute we delay could increase the odds of her killers getting away."

It was the voice of experience. Maybe not just as a Texas Ranger, either. After all, it'd taken twenty-three years for his mother to be brought to justice.

Still...

"Those fake cops were just at the sheriff's office," she reminded him. "What if they come back?"

"Then Colt and I will deal with it." He looked out the window at the sky again just as some lightning zipped across the sky. "We should get the babies in my truck before the rain starts."

Laine glanced out at the clouds, too, trying to gauge how much time they had, but Tucker cursed again and took hold of her arm to push her behind him. The movement was so sudden that she couldn't figure out why he'd done it.

Then Laine looked over his shoulder and out the window.

Her heart dropped to her knees.

There were two men, dressed in blue cop uniforms, walking across the pasture directly toward the house.

Chapter Three

Tucker didn't consider that he might be going out on a limb by assuming the two men stalking toward his house were also the men who'd killed a woman in cold blood.

Well, if she had indeed been murdered.

But believing that wasn't much of a stretch, either. Laine had arrived at his place, scared out of her mind. She must have thought a murder had taken place and that the danger still existed.

These men could be proof of it.

They were both wearing sidearms, both shifting their gazes from one side of the pasture to the other. Keeping watch. Something lawmen would do.

Criminals, too.

The one on the right pointed toward the ground. Probably because he'd spotted Laine's footprints. Too bad the rain hadn't hit to wash them away, because her tracks led right to his back door.

"Oh, God," Laine mumbled, and she just kept repeating it until he was certain she was losing it.

"Get back in the pantry," Tucker ordered her.

He took out his phone to call Colt, but it would take his brother at least twenty-five minutes to get from town to this part of the ranch.

Hell.

That was too long, so he tried to figure out a faster solution.

His other brother, Cooper, wasn't at the main house because he was away on his honeymoon. That would have been his best bet, since Cooper could have gotten to Tucker's house in just a couple of minutes. Without that option, he had to call someone he didn't want to see.

His sister Rayanne.

She was a deputy sheriff on a leave of absence, and by all accounts, she was solid at her job. But since his twin sisters, Rayanne and Rosalie, had been raised by his mother, the girls were on their mom's side when it came to this trial.

Tucker wasn't anywhere near that side.

And that had made for plenty of tense moments in the past couple of weeks since Jewell, his sisters and his stepbrother, Seth, had arrived at the ranch. Because Jewell owned Sweetwater Ranch, he and his brothers hadn't been able to turn them away, but there hadn't been any warm welcomes, either.

However, for now Tucker had to put that bad blood and ill will aside and find a backup. Even if it meant turning to a sibling or a stepsibling who disliked him as much as he disliked them.

Tucker quickly scrolled through the numbers. He tried Rayanne first. He didn't have her cell number, but unlike Rosalie and Seth, she was staying in the main house.

His home.

Because Rayanne had reminded everyone that it was her home, too.

Yeah, calling her wouldn't be much fun.

Mary, the housekeeper, answered, and Tucker asked

her to buzz Rayanne's room. He said a quick prayer that she'd be there and not out visiting Jewell all the way over at the county jail.

"What?" Rayanne answered, sounding about as friendly as Tucker felt.

"I have a situation. Two armed men posing as cops are approaching my house. They're possibly killers...." And here was the hard part. He glanced back at Laine's bleached complexion and the baby she was holding.

No, not that hard. Two babies' lives could be at stake.

"I need your help," he told Rayanne.

Tucker expected her to ask him for more details, tell him a flat-out no, or at least hesitate.

She didn't.

"I'll be right there. Don't shoot me by mistake," Rayanne snarled.

He figured that last part was an insult to his skills as a Texas Ranger, but he didn't care how many barbs Rayanne slung at him. He only needed a warm body who knew how to shoot just in case this came down to a gunfight.

"If you have another gun, I can help," Laine offered.

"No." He didn't want the babies left alone, and he didn't think it was a good idea to give an already shaky woman a gun that she might not even know how to use. "Stay where you are, and if I tell you to get down, do it."

That didn't put any color back in her face, but she nodded and stayed put.

"Where are the men now?" Laine asked. "What are they doing?"

"They're still following your tracks." They were taking slow, easy steps, and only one of them had his attention on the house.

The other was doing the tracking.

Tucker mumbled some profanity when the men drew their guns, and he debated what he could do to try and diffuse the situation. He should probably identify himself as a lawman, but if they were indeed killers, they'd just try to eliminate him so they could get to Laine and the babies.

Then they'd eliminate her.

After all, they'd followed her here, which meant they knew she'd either witnessed the murder or had some knowledge about it or the dead woman.

And that made Laine a loose end.

The seconds ticked with each step the men took, and every inch of him became alert. Tucker had been in situations like this. Facing down suspected killers and waiting for an attack that might or might not happen. But the stakes had never been this high. He had two newborns to protect.

One of the men suddenly stopped, his gaze zooming to the back part of the property. No doubt the route that Rayanne would be taking.

Had they seen her?

If so, he hoped his sister had taken some basic precautions so she wouldn't get herself shot. He suspected she hadn't when the other man pivoted in that direction. Tucker knew he couldn't wait. He had to do something to make sure they didn't gun Rayanne down.

He reached over and opened the door just a fraction so he could see out. "I'm Tucker McKinnon, Texas Ranger," he shouted to them.

Like his earlier call to Rayanne, Tucker wasn't sure what response he'd get from them. But the men stopped and lowered their guns.

That was a good start.

"I'm Sergeant Floyd Hines," the one on the left answered. In his late twenties or early thirties, he was heavily muscled and had nondescript brown hair. "And this is my partner, Detective Norman Hacker." He was on the lean side, with a mean-looking scar running down his cheek.

"We traced a fugitive here," Hines added.

Tucker had to hand it to them—they sure sounded like cops. And maybe they were. Dirty ones. Because he already knew they weren't SAPD.

The rain started. Tucker stayed to the side of the door so they could still hear him, without him needing to put himself in the direct line of fire.

"What fugitive?" he asked the men.

"Laine Braddock. She assisted in helping a federal prisoner escape."

Laine made a sound of outrage, but Tucker motioned for her to stay quiet. Maybe the babies would do the same.

"She's not here," Tucker lied. "You need to be on your way."

The men exchanged glances, obviously not pleased with his lack of cooperation.

"Where is she?" Hines asked, in the way a cop would ask. A demand rather than a question.

"Wouldn't know. I'm not exactly on friendly terms with her."

Hines mumbled something to his partner that Tucker couldn't hear. "We have reason to believe she's inside your house," Hines continued. "We're coming in to check."

Well, they weren't short of gall. But then neither was Tucker. "You got a search warrant?"

That earned him scowls from both of them. "We figured you'd cooperate with your brothers in blue."

"Not this time. Come back when you've got that warrant." Tucker shut the door and kept watch out the window.

The pair definitely didn't turn and leave. They stood there mumbling and looking around for what seemed an eternity. That eternity screeched to a halt when one of the babies started crying.

Not a whimper, either.

A full-fledged cry. Worse, the other one started to cry, too. No way could those men miss that.

Hines raised his gun again and started toward the house. He was no longer moving at a cautious pace. He began to run as if he planned to ram right through the back door.

"Wouldn't do that if I were you," someone shouted.

Rayanne.

Hacker pivoted in her direction. Fired. The shot blasted through the air, and he dropped to the ground behind a tree. Hopefully Rayanne had gotten down, as well.

"Stay on the floor, as low as you can get," Tucker warned Laine again, and he threw open the door so he could return fire.

Hines bolted behind Tucker's truck. That didn't stop the man from shooting, though. This time, the bullet smacked into the door less than an inch from where Tucker was standing.

Hell's bells.

So, he had his confirmation.

These guys were killers, and they were firing shots into a house where they knew Laine and the babies were hiding.

"Don't go out there," Laine whispered as Tucker stooped down and opened the door a little farther.

"I can't let them keep shooting into the house." And anyway, Rayanne was out there. Responding to his call for backup. He didn't intend to let her face down these guys alone.

Laine continued to protest, but the sounds of the babies' cries and the shots drowned her out. Tucker created some sounds of his own by sending a shot at Hines. The bullet smacked into Tucker's truck, very close to his intended target, but the miss got him the results he wanted.

Hines leaned over to fire again.

And this time, Tucker made sure he didn't miss.

He didn't go for a kill shot. He wanted this dirtbag alive so he could explain what the heck was happening here, so Tucker shot Hines in the right shoulder. When the idiot still kept hold of his gun, Tucker put another bullet in his arm.

Even over the noise of the gunfight, Tucker heard Hines groan in pain, and he finally let go of his gun.

Hacker cursed. No doubt because he realized his partner had been shot and was now unable to return fire. Rayanne gave him another reason to spew some profanity. Tucker saw her dart out from behind one of the trees and take aim at Hacker.

"Drop your gun now!" she ordered.

Tucker hurried onto the small porch and took aim at Hacker, as well. A single word of profanity left the man's mouth before he tossed his gun to the side and lifted his hands in surrender.

"Get on the ground," Tucker demanded. "Both of you."

Hines's arm and shoulder were bleeding, and he was clearly in pain, but he eased himself to the ground. About fifteen yards away, Hacker did the same.

Tucker slid his phone across the floor toward Laine. "Call Colt and tell him to get out here now. We'll need an ambulance, too."

Laine gave a shaky nod, and even though she now had both babies in her arms, she managed to grab the phone.

Since Tucker figured the two gunmen could be carrying backup weapons anywhere on their bodies, he kept his own gun aimed and ready when he made his way out the door and down the porch steps. Rayanne kept her gun ready, too, and went to Hacker. Tucker went to Hines.

"Colt should be here soon," Tucker relayed to Rayanne. But maybe he could use the time to figure out who these guys really were.

Tucker took aim at Hines's head. "Start talking. Tell me about the woman you killed."

"Didn't kill nobody," the man snarled. He had his hand clamped to his arm, the pain etched all over his face, but he still managed to look cocky and defiant.

"Wrong answer. Try again." Tucker made sure he sounded cocky, too. "Who sent you here?"

His tobacco-stained teeth came together in a sneer. "Even if I knew that, I wouldn't tell you. Wouldn't be good for my health."

"Neither is bleeding out." Though the man didn't seem to be in danger of doing that, Tucker took his threat a little further. "I can get an ambulance out here real fast. Or real slow. Your choice."

His mouth tightened even more. "You're not gonna let me die."

No. But Tucker figured he could bluff him into thinking otherwise. "You just took shots at me, my sister and a friend of mine."

"She ain't no friend of yours. I know who she is. And

who you are. I know that your mama killed her daddy, and there's bad blood between you two. No reason to protect her."

"I'm a *real* lawman," Tucker snapped.

That only deepened the man's sneer.

The rain started to come down harder. The thunder rumbled, too. Maybe that ambulance would get there before one of them got hit by lightning.

"You don't need this guy alive, do you?" Rayanne called out. She was standing over Hacker, her gun aimed right at him, while he wriggled belly-down on the ground.

"Why'd you ask that?" Tucker wanted to know.

"Because he's got that look, that's why. The one that morons get right before they do something really stupid, like try and go for my gun. If he does, I want to make sure it's okay for me to put some bullets in his head."

The *moron* quit moving.

"We don't need him alive," Tucker assured her.

And that wasn't exactly a bluff. Of course, he would prefer both men breathing so he could try to pit them against each other during the interrogations, but since Hacker's shots could have hurt those newborns, Tucker wasn't feeling very charitable toward the man.

Or toward Hines.

Hines was on his back on the ground. Tucker put his boot against the man's throat. "Talk. Tell me why you came here for Laine."

"Laine," he repeated. "Sounds as if you two have mended some fences."

Not exactly. But being caught in a gunfight together had a way of pushing those old issues to the side.

For a little while anyway.

"Mending fences won't save her," Hines said. His top

lip lifted. It was more sneer than smile, but the warning put a knot in Tucker's gut.

So did the sound.

Behind them, in the house, Tucker heard something he sure didn't want to hear.

Laine's shout.

"Tucker! There's another gunman."

Chapter Four

Laine saw the third man. But it was seconds too late to try to get the babies out of the house. Too late to do anything other than call out to Tucker and hope that would be enough to save them.

The hulking goon must have come in from the front of the house, away from the fight that'd been going on in the side yard with Tucker, his sister and the other two killers.

"Don't do anything stupid," the man warned her. He stepped into the doorway of the pantry, blocking her exit, and pointed a gun right at her.

Just the sight of him caused the skin to crawl on the back of her neck, but Laine forced herself not to panic. She had the babies gripped in her arms, but she put them back on the floor so she could position herself in front of them. Trying to protect them while she prayed that Tucker would get there fast enough to put a stop to this.

If Tucker was able to do it, that is.

She'd heard those shots outside, and one of them could have hit Tucker before he even made it out to stop the gunmen. It sickened her to think of that. She hadn't wanted to involve him or his sister in this, but she'd had no choice.

Laine didn't recognize the guy in front of her, but he was huge. At least six foot four and with a hulking body and wide shoulders. Even if he hadn't had the gun, he would have been formidable.

"The three of you are coming with me," the man snarled, and he used the barrel of his gun to motion for her to get moving. "Now!" he added when she didn't budge.

Laine couldn't risk him firing, because even if he didn't intend to hurt the babies, it could easily happen in such a confined space.

"Please don't hurt them." Not that she thought pleading would help, but it might be able to buy her some time.

Or not.

"I said move!" he shouted.

The man came right at her, caught onto her arm and flung her against the pantry shelves. Her shoulder hit the shelves hard, and the pain jolted through that entire side of her body. In the back of her mind, Laine realized she'd have bruises. Too bad worse things could happen in the next couple of minutes.

Boxes of pasta and canned soup tumbled off the shelves, pelting the floor. Despite the hard grip the man still had on her, Laine dropped back down so she could prevent the babies from being hit.

She didn't stay there long. Once the pantry items had stopped falling, she did the only thing she could do. She came up fighting.

Laine grabbed the first thing she could reach—a large can of mixed nuts—and threw it at him. It hit him on the chin, the can flying open, flinging nuts at him, but the can and nuts bounced off him as if he hadn't even felt it.

She didn't stop. She hurled a can of soup at him next, and received the same reaction as before. Well, almost. She hadn't thought it possible, but the fury in his expression actually went up a notch.

Making a feral growling sound, he came after her again.

But he froze. Then cursed. Without warning, he caught onto her hair and hauled her out of the pantry and into the kitchen.

She heard them then.

The footsteps.

With his gun gripped in his hand, Tucker came in from the living room and took cover by the partial wall that divided the kitchen from the rest of the house. Maybe he'd tried to sneak up on the guy, but if so, it hadn't worked. The man dragged her in front of him and put the gun to her head.

She was now a human shield.

"Put down your gun," Tucker ordered him. Rainwater dripped from his hair and clothes. "Your *friends* are cuffed in the yard, and my sister's guarding them. Or maybe she's killing them," he added. "More backup will be here in a few minutes."

Despite having a gun to her head, relief flooded through Laine. Well, temporarily anyway. The other killers had been caught, and now this guy was the only one left standing. Hopefully not for long, though. Tucker needed to arrest them all so she could find out about the woman these monsters had murdered.

"You won't make it out of here alive," Tucker told the man. He stayed behind cover, using his left hand to bracket his shooting wrist.

"Oh, yeah? With those kids and her, I believe I will," he growled.

Laine could no longer see her captor's expression, but she could certainly see Tucker's. Every muscle in his body was hard and tight. He was a lawman ready for the fight, but this was a fight they could all lose if she somehow didn't manage to protect the babies.

"Escaping with newborns will be tricky at best," Laine reminded the man. "You can take just me and move faster." Not that she especially wanted to play the martyr here, but she didn't have many options.

Obviously, her *option* didn't please Tucker because he shot her a glare. Laine ignored it. If she could do anything to change her captor's mind, she would.

"Taking me and me alone is your best option for staying alive and escaping," she added. "The babies would just slow you down."

She got exactly the reaction she'd expected. Another glare from Tucker when he glanced over at her.

"Laine, if you want to get out of this big hole, you need to stop digging," Tucker warned her. "He doesn't want to take an innocent woman."

"Innocent?" the guy growled. "Yeah, right. You might wanta check your facts there, bud. She's a lot of things, but innocent ain't one of them."

Tucker's glare faded, and for a split second he got a confused look on his face. "What the heck does that mean?"

She couldn't be sure, but Laine thought the guy might be smiling. "It means you need to ask her."

"I'd rather stop you," Tucker fired back. "The questions and answers can come later."

If she made it out of this, and it was a big if, then she obviously had some explaining to do. But for now, Laine had to get the gunman away from the babies.

"Okay," the gunman finally said, "it's just you and me, darlin'. And if you try anything funny, your cowboy here is gonna be the one who pays. Got that?"

That was the only warning Laine got before the man hooked his arm around her neck. He kept the gun pressed to her head.

"Just so you know, cowboy," the man drawled. "I got no problem putting a bullet in her, or you for that matter, so my advice is for you to back off."

Tucker stayed put. But the man maneuvered her forward, each step taking him farther away from the babies. She couldn't see them, but they definitely weren't asleep. Laine could hear them making some whimpering sounds, and she prayed everything was okay.

"This way." Her captor didn't lead her toward the kitchen door, where Tucker's sister was likely holding his comrades. Instead, he dragged her forward, which meant they'd have to go right past Tucker.

Tucker adjusted, moving just out of the guy's reach, but his gun stayed trained on him.

"You're not going to get far on foot," Tucker said. "Especially not with the storm moving in."

The man shook his head. "Won't need to go far."

Maybe because he had a vehicle stashed nearby. But more likely it was because he intended to kill her once he'd used her to escape.

No way would he want to keep her alive, since she'd witnessed the murder.

Even if he hadn't been the one to pull the trigger, he would still be charged as an accessory, which carried the same sentence. He was looking at the death penalty if she stayed alive and could testify against him.

Behind her, the babies began to cry. She desperately wanted to go to them and try to comfort them, but each step she took kept the killer away from them. That's why

Laine didn't resist when the goon practically dragged her past Tucker and toward the front of the house.

Tucker followed, of course. Using the furniture for cover along the way, he kept his attention pinned to the man. They went through the small dining area and into the living room. Without taking the gun from her head, he reached behind him and opened the front door.

Laine immediately felt the dampness of the rain, and even over the sound of it on the tin roof and the babies' cries, she heard something else. Sirens in the distance.

Backup was on the way.

The man's arm stiffened, and he mumbled some profanity. Still, that didn't stop him maneuvering her onto the porch with him.

There were six limestone steps leading down into the yard. A fence and gate, too, and some woods on the other side of the narrow road.

Those woods were no doubt where he intended to take her. And kill her. That meant she had to do something in the next few seconds.

But what?

She looked at Tucker to see if he could give her a suggestion, but he only shook his head. "Sooner or later, this clown will make a mistake, and I'll take the kill shot," Tucker said.

"You wish," the guy growled.

His choke hold on her neck got even tighter, and he began to back down the steps with her. Escaping would take precious time, and with sirens moving closer with each passing moment, Laine could feel the gunman's muscles getting tenser.

He was trapped.

"Maybe you could get a plea bargain," she suggested.

"Maybe you could shut up!"

The moment he cleared the steps, the rain began to swipe at them. Either the rain was cold for September, or it was just her nerves, but Laine immediately started shivering. Unlike Tucker. He was using the doorjamb for cover, but there were no signs that this was anything but routine for him.

Again, the man reached behind them and opened the gate, pulling her through the opening and onto the road. Because of the way he was holding her, she couldn't turn her head, but from the corner of her eye, she saw flashes of blue lights approaching.

It wouldn't be long before backup was in place and ready to help, but Laine didn't know if that would make the situation better or worse. She could feel her captor's anxiety soaring even higher.

The man continued to move, dragging her across the road and directly toward the woods. He didn't stop even when a Sweetwater Springs cruiser braked a few yards away. Colt got out, using the car door for cover, and took aim at her captor. Too bad Colt didn't have any better chance than Tucker did.

Just up the road from the cruiser, there was another set of lights and a siren. An ambulance. However, unlike Colt, the driver stayed back, no doubt waiting until it was safe enough to approach.

"If you get a shot, take it," Tucker told his brother.

"Yeah, do that," the man snarled. "It's a good way to get the shrink here killed. I'm thinking if you shoot me, my trigger finger will automatically tense up. And boom, there she goes."

Laine's shoes sank into the ground when he dragged her off the road and onto the soft shoulder. Just a few steps from the woods. It was now or never. If she didn't try to do something, he'd escape with her.

It was a huge risk, but Laine drew back her elbow and rammed it into his stomach. He cursed at her, calling her a name, and she jabbed him again. All the while, she braced herself in case he chose to retaliate.

He did.

The man pulled the trigger, and the pain immediately crashed through her head.

Laine nearly went to her knees. It took a moment—one terrifying moment—to realize he hadn't shot her. The pain was from the excruciating noise of the bullet being fired so close to her ear. But Laine felt no relief at being spared, because she had no idea where that bullet had landed.

Tucker jumped to the side, still ready to return fire. He didn't appear to be hurt. Neither was Colt. But the shot could have gone into the house. That gave her a much-needed jolt of adrenaline, and she started fighting. At least if he shot her, Tucker would be able to kill the guy.

"This isn't over," he growled.

He shoved her, hard. So hard that Laine stumbled forward and fell at the edge of the road.

"Stay down, Laine!" Tucker warned her, a split second before he pulled the trigger.

Tucker scrambled to the ground near her, but he lifted his hand to fire again. Laine tried to see if he'd managed to shoot the guy, but Tucker pushed her right back down.

Then he cursed.

"He's getting away," Tucker mumbled.

Laine's first reaction to that was, *No!* But at least if he was running, it meant he wouldn't be firing shots into the house. Of course, the downside to that was that if he escaped, he could come after her and the babies again.

"Be careful," Tucker said, and it took her a moment to realize why he'd issued that warning. It was meant for his brother.

With his gun ready, Colt bolted from the side of the cruiser and went after the man.

"The babies," Laine reminded him. "They're in the house alone." And while Tucker had said that his sister had contained the other two men, they could always try to escape and go inside to take the newborns.

Tucker pulled her right back down when she tried to get up, and he kept his attention pinned to the woods where Colt had disappeared. The seconds crawled by. No sounds. No shots. The gunshot had dulled her hearing, but she could feel the steady throb of her heartbeat crashing in her ears.

"Move fast," Tucker finally said, and he stood, pulling her to her feet.

Laine didn't even have time to regain her balance before he started running with her toward the house. Tucker got her up the steps and inside, and then he shut the door.

The babies were still crying, and Laine tried to go to them. Again Tucker moved in front to stop her. He was still the vigilant lawman, his gaze still firing all around.

Mercy, was there another gunman in the house?

They moved slowly, with Tucker checking every corner until they worked their way to the kitchen.

"Stay here," he insisted.

With his gun ready, he first looked out the kitchen window where his sister and the other two men still were. Everything must have been okay there because he started to check out the rest of the house.

Laine hurried to the babies to make sure they were okay. They appeared to be. Since she was soaked to the bone, she put the blanket between the babies and her wet clothes before she scooped them into her arms.

Even though they were too young to understand, they were perhaps sensing the horrible nightmare that'd just happened. She tried rocking them so they would stop crying and she could hear what was going on in the house.

It seemed to take an eternity for Tucker to return, and when she saw him, Laine released the breath she'd been holding. He no longer had his gun raised, and there was some relief in his eyes.

"Are you okay?" he asked. "Did he hurt you?"

"I'm fine," Laine lied. Her scrapes and bruises would all be minor, but it might take a lifetime or two to feel *fine*.

His phone rang, and he yanked it from his pocket. "It's Colt," he relayed to her, and he answered it.

Laine couldn't hear what his brother was saying, but she knew from his expression that it wasn't good news. "The rain washed away the tracks," Tucker explained, a muscle flickering in his jaw.

So they'd lost him.

Laine couldn't stop the sound from making its way through her throat. This wasn't over. The babies still weren't safe.

"We'll get a CSI team out to look for anything to indicate where he's heading," Tucker added, though he didn't sound convinced that it would do any good.

The man probably had a vehicle stashed nearby and was already long gone.

Tucker didn't stay in the pantry. Instead, he went to the back door, opened it and kept watch over the two gunmen they had managed to capture. He also motioned toward the ambulance, obviously giving them the go-ahead to come closer to the house. After he'd done that, he glanced back at her, and this time, there was no relief anywhere on his face.

Just questions.

Well, one question anyway.

"What the heck was that clown talking about back there?" Tucker asked.

Laine knew exactly what Tucker was referring to, and she remembered every word of what the man had said.

You might wanta check your facts there, bud. She's a lot of things, but innocent ain't one of them.

She opened her mouth. Closed it. Shook her head. Obviously that reaction didn't please Tucker, because he mumbled some profanity and snapped back around to face her.

"What did he mean?" Tucker demanded. "And what the heck are you really doing here?"

Chapter Five

Tucker had a dozen other things that he should be doing. For one thing, he should be helping Rayanne guard the two dirtbags she had facedown and cuffed on the ground in the drenching rain. For another, he needed to watch for Colt to make his way back to the house so they could transport the prisoners—one to the jail and the other to the hospital.

Instead, here he was questioning Laine.

And it was obvious from her reaction that she had something to tell him that he didn't want to hear.

"Did you lie to me when you said a woman had been killed?" he demanded.

"No!" She struggled to get to her feet. It wasn't easy with two crying, squirming babies in her arms. "I saw her, and they murdered her."

She sounded convincing enough, but Tucker would wait for some evidence. Still, it wasn't much of a stretch to believe it now that the attack had happened here. Those goons had been trying to cover up something, that was for sure.

"Then, what did the man mean about you not being innocent?" Tucker pressed.

She swallowed hard. "Remember when you had me fired from the undercover investigation?"

He nearly reminded her again that he'd merely asked that she be reassigned because of their old baggage. His supervisor had agreed with him. End of story.

Except it obviously wasn't.

"What'd you do?" Tucker asked, once he got his teeth unclenched.

"The case was important to me," she said, her chin coming up in a defiant pose. Just as quickly, it came down, and she dodged his gaze. "I didn't want to just drop it because you and I couldn't get along. I wanted to help find those women and babies."

Yeah, so had he.

By all accounts, there were dozens of missing women and babies lost in the maze of a massive black-market baby ring. Not just illegal adoptions, but illegal surrogacies, as well. Even pregnant women who were kidnapped until their babies were born, at which point the new mothers were murdered.

Cooper had helped to uncover and shut down a baby farm. That was a start. But there was evidence of many other farms.

And just as many cold-blooded killers operating them.

"Please tell me you didn't do anything dangerous or stupid," Tucker said.

Laine sure didn't jump to tell him that she hadn't. Which meant she had.

Tucker groaned. "What'd you do?" he repeated.

"I used some of the criminal informant contacts from the investigation to try to find another baby farm." She paused, her gaze coming back to his. "And I found one."

"Where?" But unfortunately Tucker had to wave off her answer when he heard a soft whistle.

It was Colt.

And the whistle was a signal they'd used since they were kids playing cops and robbers. It was just to let Tucker know he was approaching so he wouldn't mistake him for a bad guy. Or in this case, shoot him.

Tucker glanced back and spotted Colt making his way across the road. His brother wasn't headed inside the house with them, but rather toward Rayanne and the prisoners.

"What's wrong?" Laine asked, and despite having both arms filled with babies, she hurried to the door beside Tucker and looked out. The medics were lifting the wounded prisoner into the ambulance.

"Rayanne, can you ride in the ambulance and keep an eye on this guy?" Tucker asked. "Colt and I will get someone else there shortly, but first I need to settle some things with Laine."

"Laine?" she repeated in an unfriendly tone. "As in Laine Braddock?"

Tucker nodded, knowing the confirmation wasn't going to help the venom in Rayanne's eyes. Unlike Rayanne, he didn't care much about their mother's upcoming trial, but he didn't want his dad and brothers dragged into it. The Braddocks, especially Laine's mother, had threatened to do just that. She'd tossed around plenty of accusations about obstruction of justice and tampering with evidence.

All unfounded and untrue.

So basically Tucker was caught in the middle. Not a comfortable place to be, especially with Laine right by his side and an estranged sister snarling at both of them.

"You mean you called me out here to save her sorry butt?" Rayanne spat out.

"Not just her," Tucker explained. "She had two newborns with her. Even you wouldn't refuse to help little babies."

Despite the rain and storm winds lashing at her, Rayanne stood there, glaring at him. Glaring at Laine, too, since she was now peering over Tucker's shoulder.

"Let me guess," Rayanne snapped, shifting her glare back to Tucker. "They're your kids?"

Now it was time for Tucker to give her an eye roll. "I'm not exactly the daddy type, now, am I? No, these are babies that Laine rescued."

He hoped.

If he was to believe anything their attacker said, then it was a strong possibility that Laine hadn't told him the truth about the babies. Or about anything else.

Still grumbling something under her breath, Rayanne followed the medics into the ambulance.

"Thank you for helping," Laine called out to her. Not a good thing to say. Anything at this point would have been unwise, especially anything coming from Laine, because it earned her another nasty glare from Rayanne.

"I'll call for more backup," Colt said, getting the second man into his cruiser. "I'm guessing Laine and the babies need a doctor, too?"

"Yeah." At least for a checkup. "I'll drive them to the hospital."

"But what about the missing gunman?" Laine asked the moment Tucker shut the door. "He could follow us into town and attack us again."

"He could, but it's my guess he's in regroup mode. And that means you need to tell me everything you did to cause these goons to come after you. Start with that criminal informant who helped you find the baby farm."

Tucker motioned for her to start talking while he went to the doors and locked them. He didn't intend to be in the house for long, but he also wanted to take a few precautions in case he was wrong about his regroup theory.

Laine didn't jump to answer, something that put a knot the size of Texas in his gut. Tucker motioned for her to get on with it.

"The criminal informant was Gerry Farrow, and he took me to the baby farm," Laine finally said. "He made me wear a blindfold so I couldn't see where we were going, and he drove around for a long time. In circles, I'm sure, so I wouldn't be able to find the place later."

His groan didn't help hush the babies any. "And you thought it was a good idea for a civilian to go walking into something like that with a person you didn't even know if you could trust?"

She glanced away again. "I wanted to find those pregnant captives and save them. I didn't want their babies sold like cattle. And I thought I had a better chance of getting in there than the cops, Rangers or FBI." Laine paused. "I saw two women, including the one who was killed in the parking lot."

Oh, man. "Funny you didn't mention that connection right off the bat. You've told the FBI all of this?"

"I told them about the baby farm, but by the time we were able to work out where it was, it was too late. When they got there, the guards and the pregnant women were all gone."

No surprise there. "You were lucky those guards didn't kill you at the farm."

She made a soft sound of agreement. "I pretended to be a potential buyer for one of the babies."

"And they believed you?" Tucker asked, not bothering to hold back on the skeptical tone in his voice. He motioned for her to follow him to the bedroom so he could do something about their wet clothes.

Laine nodded. Then she lifted her shoulder. "They didn't try to kill me, anyway. They made some calls, did a quick background check and learned that I had indeed been trying to adopt."

Tucker hadn't thought there could be any more surprises today, but he'd been wrong. "You did a fake adoption request for the sake of the investigation?"

"No," she snapped. That put some fire in her ice-blue eyes, but it quickly cooled down. "I can't have children, so I've been trying to adopt for months now."

In a town the size of Sweetwater Springs, it was hard to keep secrets, but Laine had obviously managed to keep that one.

And it caused him to curse again.

"You gave those guards your real name?" The babies didn't like his near shout, and they fussed even louder.

"I figured that was the fastest way to get them to believe I was really there looking for a baby."

There were so many things wrong with that comment that Tucker didn't know where to start. "So, you let them believe you were a customer willing to break the law. Obviously that didn't work out so well, did it?"

"Obviously," she mumbled. "One of the guards told me they'd be in touch, and we left. But they did follow us."

Of course they did.

Tucker rummaged through his closet, locating some dry clothes for himself and a white button-up shirt for

Laine. He dropped it all on the dresser. He also maneuvered her away from the window and helped her put the babies on the bed so she could change.

"They followed you to your office?" he asked.

But he darn near forgot the question when Laine shucked off her wet top. She had on a lacy white bra, but the rain had practically made it see-through.

This wasn't the kid he'd kissed in his granddaddy's kitchen.

Nope. Laine was a fully grown woman now, with real curves he had no business gawking at. She obviously felt the same because she scowled when she noticed where his attention had landed.

"Sorry, I forgot we had this…connection between us," she mumbled.

"There's nothing between us," Tucker jumped to say.

Too bad it was a big fat lie. One that he had zero intention of straightening out. He yanked off his shirt as if he'd waged war on it.

"To answer your question—no, the guards didn't follow me," she snapped.

Because his mind still wasn't where it should be, it took him a moment to remember the question—had the guards followed the CI and her back to her office?

"How would you know if they'd followed you there or not?" he pressed.

Laine huffed, snatched up the shirt. The moment she had it on, she eased down on the bed beside the babies, trying to comfort them. "The CI made sure of that. He drove around with me until they stopped following us, and he said it was safe."

"Well, he was clearly wrong about that, wasn't he?" He

huffed. "Remember, there are two things that make a CI. Being a paid informant and being a criminal."

"What does that mean?"

Her gaze snapped back to his. Probably something she wished she could take back, because Tucker had already stripped down to his boxers. Proving that she was the most stubborn woman in the whole state of Texas, she didn't look away.

"It means the CI could have been looking for a way to earn a few bucks. He could have gone back to the baby farm and told them that he was suspicious of you and that you needed to be taken care of."

Laine opened her mouth, no doubt to deny that, but then she shook her head. Her eyes widened, and she touched her fingers to her mouth. "Oh, God."

"Yeah, *oh, God,*" he mumbled. "You took a serious risk going out there, going anywhere, with that idiot. And even if he was truly trying to help, he put your neck right on the line by taking you into a hornet's nest."

He could have continued his tirade for several more minutes, but his phone rang, and Tucker saw Reed's name on the screen. He hoped the deputy had some good news, because they sure as heck needed it. He hit the speaker button so he could take the call and finish dressing.

"I was just out at the parking lot behind Laine's office," Reed said. "I found some blood."

Tucker cursed, not because he hadn't expected the news. After everything Laine had told him, he had, but that blood was confirmation they were dealing with killers and not just some loons out to kidnap a pair of newborns.

"There's not much blood left because it's raining hard," Reed went on. "Still, I found some spots on the corner of the building beneath the eaves. Found a pacifier, too. Hard to tell, but it might have a fingerprint on it. DNA, too, if the rain hasn't gotten to it."

"Send it and the blood sample to the Ranger lab for immediate processing," Tucker instructed. He glanced at the babies. He needed to know who the dead woman was so he could locate the babies' next of kin.

"Any security cameras nearby?" Tucker asked. "Maybe we can get footage of what happened. In case we don't have a print, we might be able to get some photos of her."

And photos of her killers, as well.

After all, Laine had said they'd gotten out of the car to retrieve the body, and that meant a camera could show the murder in progress.

"Maybe," Reed answered. "That new jewelry store up the street has cameras. Don't know if the angles are right, but I'll call them while I'm driving out to check Laine's car for prints."

"Make the call, but skip the fingerprints on the car for now." With the rain, it was probably a lost cause anyway. Besides, he had something more important for Reed to do. "Come out to my place. I'd like someone close by in case things get ugly again."

That didn't help soothe any of the tension from Laine's face. It wouldn't help soothe his, either, but it was a precaution Tucker needed to take.

Not just for Laine, but for those babies.

The moment he finished the call with Reed, Laine said, "The dead woman could have heard the guards or the CI mention me. She could have heard my name, and that's why she called me."

Yeah, Laine's phone number wouldn't have been hard to find. But why had the woman thought she could trust

Laine? And how the heck had she gotten away from the baby farm and into town?

"She probably heard more than just your name," Tucker explained. "She likely heard the guards say that they didn't trust you, that you could be working for the cops."

Of course that meant assuming the woman was totally innocent in all of this. And that she was indeed trying to protect her babies. But maybe the men killed her for a different reason, and finding that reason would only be possible if they first learned her identity. Hopefully the blood Reed had found would help with that.

"Come on." Tucker grabbed some towels from the adjoining bathroom. "Reed will be here soon, and I need to get the babies and you to the hospital for checkups."

Laine gave a shaky nod, probably because she wasn't thrilled about going outside, where the missing gunman might spot her. "And then what?"

"Protective custody. A safe house."

Another nod. She wrapped the babies each in the towels. Not ideal cover, but it was better than using the damp blanket Laine had used to hold them earlier.

"Can you manage to carry both of them?" he asked. It was a strange question, because she'd carried them across the pasture to get to his house, but she was more shaken up now. After all, she'd just come darn close to dying.

"Yes." And her attention went to the belt holster he'd just put on. Then to the backup weapon he slid into the back of his jeans.

"I'll pull the truck right up to the steps," he assured her. "By the time we make it to the road, Reed should be here."

Tucker had barely made it a step before he heard the sound of a car engine. He hurried to the front window, expecting to see Reed's truck, but it was a black four-door sedan.

"What's wrong?" Laine asked, obviously noticing the change in his body language.

"Maybe nothing." Of course, it felt like something since it could be their attacker returning.

However, the man who stepped out from the car wasn't the escaped gunman. This guy was in his late twenties and had pale blond hair. He was wearing a dark gray suit, with no sign of a weapon. He ducked his head against the storm and ran toward the porch.

The man wasn't alone. There was someone else in the car, but Tucker could only make out a silhouette because of the rain-streaked windows.

"You know him?" Laine asked.

"No. Wait here and stay away from the windows." Tucker didn't move until she had the babies back by the bed before he drew his gun and started for the door. Their visitor knocked just as he got there. He swung open the door and asked the guy to identify himself.

"Martin Hague," the man said, but his voice trailed off to nothing but breath when he spotted Tucker's gun. "I heard on the drive over that you'd had some trouble out here."

"Who'd you hear it from?" Tucker demanded, and he didn't even try to sound friendly.

"A nurse who works at the hospital. Someone from the ambulance called ahead and said they were bringing in a man who'd been wounded here. Good thing I was already on my way to your place."

"Who the heck are you?" Yet another demand.

"Oh, I'm from social services." He reached for his pocket, but he stopped when Tucker lifted his gun. "Just getting my ID." He didn't continue until Tucker gave him the nod, and then he extracted a leather case with his credentials.

It looked official, but Tucker wasn't taking any chances. He didn't lower his gun. "What do you want?"

"I'm a social worker," Hague said, as if the answer were obvious.

He took out a piece of paper and handed it to Tucker just as the other person stepped from the car. A man wearing a uniform and badge that Tucker instantly recognized. He was a Department of Public Safety officer.

"That paper should clarify everything for you," Hague said. "We're here to take the babies."

Chapter Six

Laine stayed away from the windows as Tucker had ordered, but because the babies had finally stopped fussing, she had no trouble understanding what Martin Hague had just said.

He was taking the babies.

She clutched them to her and kept listening. Laine couldn't hear every word they said, but she detected the concern in Tucker's voice. After everything they'd been through, that was probably normal, but this didn't feel normal to her.

Sweet heaven.

Laine hoped that feeling wasn't because she was starting to get attached to the babies. They weren't hers, and she couldn't keep them. Even if it squeezed at her heart to think of handing them over to this social worker.

"You don't have a court order?" Tucker asked.

That got her attention. Laine slipped out of the bedroom and into the living room so she could try to figure out what was going on.

"It's standard procedure to take minors into our protective custody when there's the possibility of danger," Hague argued. "And from what I've learned, there's also a question of the infants' paternity."

"They're already in protective custody," Tucker snapped. "*Mine.* And this is an active crime scene. The babies' clothes need to be processed for evidence. And how the devil did you find out the babies were even here?"

"Your brother, Deputy Colt McKinnon, reported that two babies had been found. We had another anonymous report that a woman had fled an abusive situation with her newborn twins."

Laine inched closer, and as if he sensed she was there, Hague's attention zoomed past Tucker and landed on her.

Or rather it landed on the babies.

"Are they all right? Were they hurt?" Hague moved as if to step around Tucker, but Tucker stepped directly in front of the babies, blocking Hague's path.

"They're fine," Tucker growled. "Their mother, maybe not so much. It's possible she was murdered, and I need to do DNA tests on the babies to determine who they are and if they're connected to the woman in question."

Hague seemed to ignore all of that. He kept his attention fastened to Laine. "You're the one who took them?"

"I *rescued* them." Laine could instantly see why Tucker was stonewalling this man. Maybe it was just because he was inexperienced, but there was something off about him.

"Your Ranger friend seems to think he has jurisdiction here," Hague said to her, aiming a glare at Tucker.

Tucker aimed one right back at him. He was far better at glaring than their guest. "Her Ranger friend is right. Someone just tried to kill us." He pointed to the woods across from the house. "Someone who's no doubt hiding out in there somewhere. Maybe with a long-range rifle."

Hague cast an uneasy glance over his shoulder before

his gaze whipped back to Tucker. "How soon will you release the babies?"

"When I'm finished with them and when you have that court order." Tucker stepped back and slammed the door in the man's face.

"You don't trust him?" Laine asked, inching closer so she could make sure Hague actually left. He did. The man stormed down the porch steps and got back in the car. He sped away much too fast considering the sopping wet roads.

"Right now I don't trust anyone."

Possibly even Laine herself. After all, she'd withheld information about visiting that baby farm. But then Tucker'd had plenty of reasons to distrust her before that.

He took out his phone and sent off a text. Laine only got a glimpse of it, but it appeared that Tucker was asking someone to do a background check on Martin Hague. A few days before, that would have seemed like overkill.

Now, nothing seemed to fall into that category.

"Change of plans," Tucker said. "I'll call Dr. Howland and ask him to come out and examine the babies and you. Not here, though. I'm taking the three of you to the main house where I'll have some help protecting you."

Laine was certain that he'd lost his mind. Now here was an example of overkill, or at least of a really bad idea.

"With your family?" She shook her head, not waiting for him to answer. "Tucker, they hate me. *You* hate me."

For some stupid reason she got a flash of the expression on his face when he'd seen her changing into the dry clothes. It was only a glimpse of this unwanted heat between them, but a glimpse had been enough to know.

"Okay, maybe you don't completely hate me," she amended, "but you certainly don't want me there."

No heated look this time. Just a flat one that let her know she'd stated the obvious. Before Laine could continue the argument, he took out his phone and made a call.

"Mary," he said when someone answered. Mary Larkin had been the McKinnon housekeeper for as long as Laine could remember.

Yet another person who wouldn't want Laine there.

"I've got a situation. Send someone out to pick up bottles, formula, diapers and anything else newborns need. I'll explain when I get there. Oh, and Laine Braddock will be with me…. Yeah, I know," he added a moment later. "Like I said, I'll explain everything."

"Still convinced that taking me there is a good idea?" Laine challenged when he ended the call.

"The house has a security system," he said, obviously ignoring her argument. "The ranch hands can help guard the place."

"But your family—"

"Cooper and his wife aren't there. They're on their honeymoon, and their son, Liam, is staying with his grandmother in Austin. Jewell's in jail, as you well know, and my sister Rosalie and Jewell's stepson, Seth, are in the guesthouse."

"That leaves your father and Rayanne," she immediately reminded him.

"My father won't object to me keeping you safe. I hope," he added. "And Rayanne's opinion doesn't count. She's only living in the house to irritate the rest of us and to rub it in our faces that it's her house, too."

Laine couldn't argue with the reason Rayanne was staying at the ranch. It was pretty much what she'd heard around town, though that wouldn't help with Laine's own situation.

But what would?

She couldn't take the babies and go to her place. The missing gunman could easily find her there. She definitely didn't want to turn the babies over to Hague, either. Not until Tucker and she had figured out what was going on. Her brother was the county sheriff, but he, too, was out of town and wouldn't be back for days.

That left her hiring a bodyguard of some kind.

But that would take time, and she didn't have much of that. It wouldn't be long before the babies would need to be fed, and Tucker had already made plans for that. So for now, Tucker and his family seemed to be her best short-term option.

Heaven help her.

"How long will we have to stay there?" she asked.

"Probably a lot longer than either of us want."

Heck, two minutes would qualify as way too long.

Tucker motioned for them to get moving, but then Laine stopped when her phone buzzed. She tried to balance the babies so she could retrieve her phone from her jeans pocket. She'd managed it earlier with one baby in her arms, but it wasn't possible with two.

Since the call could be important, she handed the infants to Tucker. He didn't scowl, but he did get the look of a man who was way out of his element. He shook his head and tried to hand them back, but Laine ignored him and checked the caller ID on the screen.

It was her mother, Carla.

It wasn't a call that Laine wanted to take. Their relationship was shaky at best, but by now news of the shooting was likely all over town, and her mom had heard about it.

"I'm all right," Laine answered right off the bat.

"Glad to hear that, but why in the world were you out at Tucker McKinnon's place?"

"Who told you I was at Tucker's?" she asked.

"Your sister. One of her reporter friends gave her the details of what happened. She's not happy about you being there, either, so why'd you go running to the McKinnons?"

"It's a long story." And one that she didn't want to discuss with anyone. Well, with anyone but Tucker. Strange that they were finally on the same side about something. "I'll call you later and tell you all about it—"

"A McKinnon killed your father," Carla snapped. "Don't you forget that."

Laine would have a harder time forgetting how to breathe. "I won't be here much longer." And when her mother's tirade continued, Laine worked in a hasty goodbye and pressed the end call button.

She glanced up at Tucker, expecting him to be in a hurry to hand off the babies, but he was no longer looking at the babies as if they were some alien creatures. The corner of his mouth had lifted, and both babies were quietly staring at him. He'd told his sister that he wasn't the fatherly type, but those babies suddenly looked very comfortable in his arms.

"Your mother's not happy about you being here," Tucker commented. He obviously hadn't needed to hear the conversation to know what'd taken place.

Laine made a sound of agreement. "You've no doubt heard the story of Jewell and my father from a different perspective than I have."

"But with the same results. Whitt's dead, and everything points to my mother having killed him. If she did it, then she'll pay."

"If?" Laine repeated. "You're not certain she killed him? Because this is the first I'm hearing about any doubts from you."

"Doesn't matter what I think. I just want her and the kids that she raised to be out of our lives." No longer smiling, he handed the babies back to her. "But I'm glad Rayanne was there to help."

Yes, without her, Tucker and she might be dead and the babies stolen.

"Let's go," Tucker said, and he led her into the kitchen. "Move fast and stay low," he added before he darted out into the rain to get into his truck.

He backed it up and then pulled it close until the passenger's side was almost right against the steps. He threw open the door and motioned for her to hurry.

She did.

Laine didn't want to be out in the open any longer than necessary, for fear the gunman was watching them. The moment she was inside, Tucker took off. Not speeding, as Hague had done. But driving at a slow, cautious pace, probably because they didn't have infant seats for the babies.

Tucker kept watch, his gaze firing all around, and Laine slipped low down in the seat. Despite what was waiting for her inside, she was glad when the massive white house came into view.

The place looked different. Bigger. And there were more barns and other outbuildings than she remembered. About thirty yards from the main house, another structure was going up.

"Cooper's new place," Tucker explained, following her gaze.

It made sense that his brother would want his own

house. After all, Cooper didn't just have a wife now. He was also the father of a toddler boy. Yet another McKinnon male who would no doubt grow up to hate her and her family.

Nope, she didn't feel one bit welcome.

"I'll run background checks on all the construction crew working on Cooper's house," Tucker added.

Good. Because it seemed an easy way for whoever was after them to get onto the grounds. They already had enough security issues without adding that to the mix.

As Tucker had done at his place, he parked right next to the porch. Mary immediately threw open the door and helped them into the foyer. It'd been a while since Laine had seen the woman, but she hadn't changed much, except she now had some threads of gray in her auburn hair.

"The diapers and formula will be here soon," Mary said. The look she gave Laine was frosty, but that frost didn't extend to the babies. Mary smiled and eased the newborn girl into her arms.

Laine hadn't realized just how much her arms were aching until Mary did that, but Laine still wanted to snatch the baby back. To protect both of them. Too bad she was shaking too much to do that. If Tucker hadn't been holding on to her arm, her legs might have buckled.

"This way." He took her into the adjoining living room and forced her to sit on a sofa. In the same motion, he pulled out his phone. "Colt," he said, putting the call on speaker. "Please tell me the fake cops have made a full confession so I can arrest someone."

"No confessions. In fact, they've both lawyered up, and the one in the hospital isn't saying a word. But I did get something from the one we're holding at the jail. His name isn't Hacker. It's Gene Buford. The guy had a record, so I got a match when I fingerprinted him. Anyway, he had three photos in his pocket. One was of Laine, and it looks like it was taken with a long-range camera at some kind of ranch."

"The baby farm," she said. She hadn't seen anyone snap her photo, but there had no doubt been security cameras. "Is one of the other pictures of a blonde woman?"

"Yes. Thin face, short choppy hair."

Laine pulled in her breath. "That sounds like the woman who was killed behind my office."

"That's what I figured. It's the third one that's confusing me. It's a picture of you, Tucker."

"Tucker?" Laine repeated.

She shook her head. Why did the men have a photo of him? There was no way they could have guessed she would have fled to his house. Heck, she hadn't even known that was where she'd been headed until she was actually on the road.

"Send me the photo of the woman," Tucker insisted.

It took several moments for the photo to load on the screen, and Laine got up to have a better look. It was the woman, all right, and just like that, the sickening memories of the shooting returned. The sound of the shots. The blood. The sheer violence of it all.

But she wasn't the only one who had a reaction.

Tucker groaned softly.

"You know her?" Laine asked.

Tucker nodded. "Yeah. Her name's Dawn Cowen." A muscle flickered in his jaw. "And I'm the reason she's dead."

Chapter Seven

Tucker stood in the shower of one of the ranch's guest bathrooms and let the scalding water slam against him. It didn't help. Nothing would. It was his fault that a woman was dead, and no amount of hot water was going to fix that.

The images of Dawn Cowen slammed against him, too. Yeah, she'd been mixed up at times, but all in all she was a good criminal informant, and she'd trusted him.

A big mistake on her part.

Because Tucker had been the one to ask her to assist with the baby farms investigation. And she had. Dawn had managed to get some information that had helped the FBI and Rangers find one of the farms. She had probably saved a life or two.

But not her own.

Someone was going to pay for that, but Tucker figured no one was going to pay as hard as he was. How the heck was he supposed to live with this? A woman was not only dead, but those two babies were now motherless because of him.

Cursing himself and this god-awful situation, he stepped from the shower, dried off and pulled on his jeans.

He was in midzip when he went back into his bedroom…
and quickly realized he wasn't alone.

Laine was sitting on his bed. "Before you say anything, consider just how uncomfortable I must have been
to choose coming up here to your bedroom over being
downstairs with the others."

Tucker smiled, not out of amusement, but because he
was relieved that she wasn't there to dump more bad news
on him. "Where are the babies?"

She hitched her thumb toward the hallway outside his
open door. "Sleeping in their bassinet in the kitchen. Rosalie offered to help watch them again. She's, uh, nice."

"Yeah." It'd been hard to find fault with that particular
sister. Unlike Rayanne, she didn't have a constant surly attitude. "Rosalie's own baby was kidnapped a while back.
From what she's said, she loves kids."

Good thing, too, because it'd required a lot of help to
take care of the babies. Neither Laine nor he had slept
more than an hour's stretch at a time, and it'd taken all of
them—Mary, Rosalie, Laine and him—just to get through
the night.

Tucker wasn't sure how parents managed it. The babies
might be cute and little, but they sure cried a lot. When
they weren't doing that, they drank formula, soiled their
diapers and slept, but not for any length of time.

He'd become an overnight expert in diapering a baby
boy. It required a lot more quickness and dexterity than
he'd ever figured.

Laine stood, her gaze starting at his face and going to
his zipper. Forgetting that he was still partially dressed,
he zipped up and located a shirt he'd had brought over
from his house.

Best not to stand around half-naked with Laine.

His nerves were raw. He was bone-tired. And for just a moment he allowed himself to think of how good and distracting it would feel to put his mouth on hers.

Good, yes. Distracting? That, too. But he'd end up paying a high price for that kind of kiss. Heck, he'd end up paying just for thinking about kissing her.

And for the way she snagged his attention.

No jeans for Laine today. She was wearing a pale green dress that skimmed her body and showed plenty of leg. No doubt an outfit that Reed had picked up from her house and brought out to the ranch. The deputy had obviously brought her some makeup, too, but the dark circles beneath her eyes let him know that she was just as sleep-deprived as he was.

"Want to talk about Dawn Cowen?" she asked, rubbing her hands down the sides of her dress.

He lifted his shoulder and sat on the other side of the bed so he could pull on his boots. "Not much to tell that you don't already know. She worked for me as a criminal informant, and she'd be alive if it weren't for the baby farm investigation."

"Maybe." She paused, fidgeting with her dress some more. "I read the report on her that was sitting on the desk of the office you're using downstairs—"

That brought him to his feet. "You did what?"

"I read it," she admitted, not backing down or even issuing a mild apology for snooping around. "A year ago she was helping you on a case, but then she stopped because she got pregnant."

"Obviously she didn't stop. She was probably kidnapped and held all these months at the baby farm. Months when I didn't bother checking on her."

"You couldn't have known what'd happened to her," Laine said.

"When I didn't hear from her, I should have guessed."

"Yes, because of the ESP that all you Texas Rangers have. I've heard it's standard issue, along with the white Stetson, boots, badge and jeans."

They exchanged flat looks, and Laine was the first to glance away.

"Besides," she continued, "if we're playing the blame game, then Dawn wouldn't have come literally running to my office if it weren't for the unauthorized visit the CI and I made to the baby farm."

"She obviously thought she could trust you. She sure as heck didn't come to me."

And that would haunt him for eternity. Most women held captive at the baby farms were murdered shortly after they delivered. Dawn must have been terrified, not just for her own life but for her newborn children.

Well, maybe they were both hers.

Dawn had indeed been pregnant, but Tucker couldn't rule out that maybe only one of them was hers and the other was one she'd managed to rescue.

"There wasn't anything in your report about Dawn being married or involved with anyone," Laine tossed out.

"The babies aren't mine, if that's what you're thinking."

"I didn't think that. If there'd been any possibility they were yours, you would have said something last night. And you would've given them better nicknames," she added.

It was no doubt her attempt to lighten things up some. It didn't work. Nothing would. But she was right—if they'd been his, he might have called them something better than Jack and Jill.

Okay, now he smiled. "Don't try to make this easier on me," he snarled.

She nodded as if taking that warning as gospel. Hesitated. Then huffed. "I need to figure out some other place to go. Someplace safe, of course."

"With the babies?"

She blinked. "Well, yes. I thought I'd keep them until we figure out where they belong."

"That could be as early as today. It shouldn't be hard to find out about Dawn's romantic interest or the babies' next of kin."

Of course, once the father was indeed found, it didn't mean the babies would be safe. It was possible the people behind the baby farm would want the newborns returned.

They could also want to take their revenge on Laine.

Once they had the babies, they could use them to draw her out. And it would probably work. Any woman who would risk going to a baby farm with a CI likely wouldn't think twice about surrendering herself to save two babies.

"If you take the babies away from the ranch, you could just be putting them in more danger," Tucker reminded her. "If these goons think you can reveal anything about their operation, they won't stop coming after you."

Obviously that was something Laine already knew, but she still flinched. Maybe because hearing the threat aloud really drilled it home. Her mouth trembled a little, and Tucker saw the thin veneer covering her fear.

Ah, heck.

Tears sprang to her eyes, too. She quickly blinked them back, lifted her defiant chin, but Tucker saw something he didn't want to see.

A vulnerable woman.

Usually a woman's tears would send him running in the opposite direction, but in this case, they sent him walking. Directly toward her. To pull her into his arms.

Not the brightest idea he'd ever had.

He blamed that on this stuff going on between them. Not just the stuff with the babies and the danger, but the old baggage, too. If they'd been enemies all their lives, it would have helped, but he kept going back to that time when they'd been friends.

And more.

When he was a kid, stupider than now, he'd spent some time thinking about the two of them being together for life. Not that at age eleven he'd known what life with a girl entailed. Truth was, he'd been more focused on kissing her than on anything else.

Heck, he was still focused on it.

Laine didn't push him away. Big surprise. She looked up at him. "Ironic, huh? When you woke up yesterday morning, I'll bet you never thought we'd be voluntarily touching each other."

Tucker shook his head, hoping that would clear it. It didn't work. Maybe he should try hitting it against the wall. "Who says this is voluntary?"

A short burst of air left her mouth. Almost a laugh. Then that troubled look returned to her eyes. "It's not a good idea for us to be here alone."

"No. It's not."

There. They were in complete agreement. Still, neither of them moved a muscle. Well, he moved some. His grip tightened on her a little, and those kissing dreams returned with a vengeance.

"Besides, I'm no longer your type," she added, as if that would help.

It didn't.

However, it did cause him to temporarily scowl. "How would you know my type?"

Another huff. Soft and silky, though, not rough like his. Her breath brushed against his mouth, almost like a kiss. Almost. "Everyone in town knows. Blonde, busty and not looking for commitment."

He was sure his scowl wasn't so brief that time, but the problem was he couldn't argue with what she'd said. Besides, the reminder accomplished what Laine had likely intended.

Tucker stepped back.

He figured that she'd say something smart-mouthed to keep things light, but she didn't. For a moment Laine actually looked a little disappointed that their hugging session had ended, and that was all the more reason for him not to pick it up again.

Ever.

Even if parts of him were suggesting he do just that.

No, she wasn't blonde or overly busty, and he had no idea if she was looking for commitment or not. His guess was no, especially when it came to the likes of him.

"I should check on the babies," Laine said, and she lit out of there as if he'd set her dress on fire.

Tucker followed her because he wanted to check on them, too, and then head to the ranch office that he'd been using. While he was there, he'd see what Laine had managed to get a look at while she was snooping. He really couldn't blame her for wanting to know what was going on. Nearly getting killed was a huge motivator to finding their escaped attacker.

Laine made it to the kitchen just ahead of him, and Tucker got a glimpse of Rayanne making a hasty exit. Before doing that, however, she scowled at them. Unlike his other sister, Rosalie. She greeted them and then smiled at the babies, who were in a Moses basket on the table.

No white gowns for them that morning. Someone had dressed them in pink and blue. Cute as bugs. They were cuddled against each other, sleeping side by side.

"Sorry about that," Rosalie said, her gaze going briefly to her sister, who was storming toward the guesthouse. Too bad Rayanne wouldn't stay there. "Rayanne wasn't always like she is now."

"Hard to believe," Tucker mumbled. Rosalie and Rayanne had barely been six years old when Jewell left with them. "She had a stubborn streak even as a kid."

That streak was now a mile wide.

"Well, she was always tough," Rosalie amended. "Always trying not to show how much it hurt that she didn't have a dad. Sorry," she immediately added. "Didn't mean to bring up any bad memories."

"She had a dad," Tucker pointed out. "A stepdad."

She nodded. "And he was good to us, but Rayanne could never let go of the anger of having our father toss our mother out of her home." Rosalie winced. "Sorry, again. I keep putting my foot in my mouth this morning."

Laine gave her a pat on the arm. "We all had our lives turned upside down twenty-three years ago."

"Yeah, and they just keep on turning, don't they?" Tucker grumbled. "Like a curse or something."

There'd been nothing but trouble and danger since Jewell had come back into their lives, but since he didn't want to hurt Rosalie's feelings, Tucker kept that little revelation to himself.

Besides, he had something better to occupy his attention. The babies.

It was strange, he'd never considered baby-watching to be very interesting, but it sure was now. Maybe because he thought of himself as their protector.

Temporarily, anyway.

Tucker reached down and touched his finger to Jack's cheek. The corner of his little mouth lifted. A baby smile that Laine and Rosalie had already assured him was just gas. Tucker figured they were wrong.

Hey, a kid who could pee with that kind of accuracy certainly could manage a smile, couldn't he?

"There is something you should know about Rayanne," Rosalie said in a whisper, like she was telling a secret. A secret she obviously wasn't so sure she should share. "I wouldn't bring it up, but Rayanne won't say anything, and it could cause some problems if she's called out to help with another arrest. Or an attack."

Tucker had to shake his head. "What are you talking about?"

Rosalie swallowed hard. "Shortly before we came here, Rayanne got involved with a guy who basically slept with her and then dumped her."

Well, that explained her surly mood. A little bit of the brother inside him kicked in. He had to rein in his protective instincts, though, because Rayanne wouldn't want him to even think about protecting her.

"Anyway," Rosalie went on, "this morning, Rayanne finally got around to taking a pregnancy test. It was positive. She thinks she's about three and a half months along."

Oh, man. That would be a hard blow for any woman, even one with Rayanne's alligator-thick skin.

"Where's the baby's father?" Tucker asked.

"He's dead. He was killed somewhere in Mexico."

Laine made a soft sound of sympathy. "She's had a lot come at her at once. Is there anything I can do to help?"

The shrink in her was coming out. It was like Tucker's brotherly tug, which he was ignoring.

Rosalie shook her head. "Anything any of us could say or do would just make it worse. Rayanne's never had dreams of being a mother, unlike me. I've always wanted children. So this has hit her pretty hard. The only reason I wanted you to know—"

"Was so I wouldn't call her into the middle of a gunfight," Tucker finished. "Let's hope it doesn't come down to that again."

His phone rang, startling the babies and causing them to squirm, and Tucker stepped into the adjoining family room to take the call. Laine followed him, and once Tucker saw it was Colt on the other end of the line, he put it on speaker, since this was something she probably needed to hear.

"Still no sign of our missing shooter," Colt started.

"And the other two?" Laine asked.

"Other than us getting Gene Buford's name, they're not talking, and their lawyers are making sure they stay quiet."

That wasn't good, but maybe there was a way around the mute act from the two they had in custody. Tucker could look at the lawyers themselves and see if they had any connections to those being investigated for the baby farms.

"I made some calls about the social worker, Martin Hague," he told Colt. "Nothing back on him so far, other than he really is a social worker."

"Let me guess—Hague's getting that court order to take the babies?" Tucker asked.

"He's trying," Colt answered. "That's why I've been trying to learn as much about the babies as possible. Both of them have the same blood type as Dawn Cowen, but there's nothing back on the DNA yet to determine if she was really their mother. She doesn't have a next of kin on file so I had Reed chat with some of the other CIs we use in San Antonio. Several of them said she has an aunt somewhere in the state."

"Maybe the Rangers can help track her down?" Tucker suggested.

"I'll ask, but I did find out something else from the CIs. You're not going to believe this, but Dawn was involved with Darren Carty."

Tucker groaned. Not Laine, though. She just stood there looking poleaxed, and her breathing suddenly didn't sound too level.

"My ex-fiancé," she finally mumbled.

She didn't offer more. Not that Tucker needed it. He was plenty familiar with Darren. Same age. Raised just one county apart, they'd competed against each other in high school football and then again on the rodeo circuit.

Tucker pretty much hated the guy, and it had nothing to do with the fact that Laine and Darren had been hot and heavy for a long time before they'd split up about two years before.

"What was Darren doing with someone like Dawn?" Laine asked, her voice a little shaky. "She had a lengthy juvenile record along with some arrests for petty theft and prostitution."

"Darren's apparently been involved with several women like her since you two split," Colt explained.

"But according to a couple of Dawn's friends, it wasn't just a fling. Not on her part, anyway. She was in love with Darren."

Something about that didn't fit. All right, a lot of things didn't fit, but Tucker went with the obvious one. "Then why didn't Darren or her friends report her missing?"

"Because Darren said Dawn had pulled disappearing acts before."

Yeah, Tucker knew that about her, too, but still, someone should have asked her whereabouts.

Including Tucker himself.

"I want to talk to Darren," Tucker insisted.

"Figured you would. I just got to his place, and I'll arrange to have him come in for a chat. Not sure how much he'll cooperate.... Oh, hell—"

"What's wrong?" Tucker couldn't ask fast enough.

"Tucker, you need to get out here right now. I think I found Dawn."

Chapter Eight

Laine looked out at the chaos in front of her, and her stomach tightened even more. Yes, Colt had already told Tucker and her that he'd found Dawn's body.

At her ex-fiancé's house, no less.

However, Laine hadn't realized just how many people would be at Darren's ranch. She spotted the medical examiner's van. A CSI one, too. Then Colt's squad car. Someone from the county sheriff's office was there, as well. Plus four other civilian vehicles, no doubt belonging to Darren and his ranch hands.

Or maybe to his lawyers.

Darren had to know just how much trouble he was in.

Tucker parked behind the ME's van about twenty yards from the house, but he didn't get out. Instead, he turned to her. "They haven't moved the body yet. They're still processing the scene."

She understood what he was saying—if she went outside, she would likely see Dawn. While Laine wasn't anxious to see the dead woman, she did want to hear what Darren had to say.

If he had anything to say.

So far, Darren hadn't said much to Colt, and in turn Colt hadn't volunteered anything about their investigation.

Since Darren's ranch straddled two different jurisdictions, both the county and the Sweetwater Springs cops had agreed to turn it over to Tucker and the Texas Rangers.

Something she was positive Darren wouldn't like.

The two men had never been on friendly terms, and Darren wouldn't have an easy time answering to a man he disliked.

"Stay close to me," Tucker warned her.

It wasn't his first warning of the day. There'd been plenty of them when he had tried to talk her out of coming with him, but Laine had simply reminded him that she would be able to confirm that Dawn was indeed the woman who'd been shot behind her office. That wasn't a lie. But Laine also wanted to see Darren's face when Tucker questioned him about his involvement with Dawn.

She wasn't jealous. Just confused. And more than a little worried that she'd once been engaged to a man who was now somehow involved in a murder.

Just as Tucker reached to open the door, his phone rang, and she saw Reed's name on the screen. He put the phone on speaker when he answered.

"Didn't know if you'd made it out to Carty's place yet, but I just got the background report on that social worker, Martin Hague," Reed greeted. "You want to hear the gist of it now or is this a bad time?"

"You found something?" Tucker immediately asked.

"Maybe. He appears to be living well beyond his means. He recently paid off some huge student loans and bought a house. Can't find any sign of an inheritance or anything. But I did find a connection that makes me uneasy. Remember the name Rhonda Wesson?"

"Yes," Tucker and Laine said in unison. It was Laine

who continued. "She was one of the pregnant women rescued from the first baby farm that was closed down."

"That's right. And she's Hague's cousin."

Laine tried to pick through what she remembered about Rhonda. The woman had a troubled past that included being on the run from an abusive relationship. Or so everyone believed until she'd been found at the baby farm. She delivered the child shortly after being rescued and then had given up the newborn for adoption.

"You think Hague's connected to the baby farm?" Laine asked.

"I just think it's a coincidence that I don't much like," Reed answered.

Laine made a sound of agreement. Of course, just because Hague's cousin had been a victim didn't mean he had been the one who put Rhonda on that baby farm. Still, it was a possible lead that Tucker and she would need to follow.

Well, Tucker anyway.

Laine wasn't sure just how much longer he would continue to let her tag along. Once their missing attacker was caught, Tucker would likely be in a hurry to end their association. Despite the way he'd held her in his bedroom. It'd been, well, nice.

Okay, not nice.

It'd been a *playing with fire* session that she should have never started in the first place.

"You okay?" she heard Tucker ask, and it took her a moment to realize he was talking to her. "You're breathing funny. If you're worried about seeing the body or your ex—"

"I'm not."

He just stared at her, obviously waiting for her to explain what was bothering her. Yes, Dawn's body was part of this mess going on in her head. The spent adrenaline and lack of sleep, too, along with the shocking news that her ex had a possible connection to everything that was going on.

But no way would she mention hugging and playing with fire while Reed was listening.

The town gossip mill already had enough fodder without her adding more, and she definitely didn't want it getting back to her mother that she'd landed not just under Tucker's roof but also in his arms.

"See if you can find the source of Hague's money," Tucker said to Reed. He still didn't take his attention off her, though. "And set up a meeting with Rhonda. I could be tied up here for a while."

"Tied up questioning Darren Carty," Reed supplied. "You arresting him?"

"That depends on how the next few minutes go. Call me if you learn anything else about Hague."

Tucker ended the call. "All right, what's wrong? If you're about to fall apart over seeing your ex, I need to know before you take one step from this truck."

"I look like I'm going to fall apart?" Laine wasn't positive that the falling apart wouldn't happen, but her latest troubled look had sadly been about her situation with Tucker and not about Dawn. "What if I just say this isn't about Darren, and that it's something you don't want to discuss? Would you leave it at that?"

But he didn't leave anything. Not Tucker. He studied her, his attention going from her eyes to her mouth. She saw the *aha/oh, hell* moment flash through his eyes.

"I'm sure it's just nerves," she added. "Better to think about you than what's out there."

"Yeah." He nodded, paused again. "So, should I know why you and Darren split? If I remember right, you two were just a few weeks away from saying 'I do.'"

"There's nothing wrong with your memory." Though it did surprise her that Tucker would remember *that* or any other personal thing about her.

Laine decided to say this fast. Like ripping off a Band-Aid. "I can't have children of my own. I didn't know that when we got engaged, but when I found out and told him, Darren broke things off."

Mercy, it hurt to say that. Hurt more to feel it. The ache was always there, eating away at her. Not because of her failed engagement, but because she would never give birth to the baby that she'd always wanted. The failed relationship was just salt on a wound that would never heal.

Tucker's mouth didn't exactly drop open, but it came close. "I knew Darren was an ass, but that proves it."

Laine shrugged. "He wanted a child of his own and didn't want to adopt. I can't fault a man for that."

"Well, I sure as hell can." He cursed. But then he went still, and Laine knew why. "Hell," Tucker repeated.

"The babies that Dawn had with her could be Darren's," she managed to say. That hurt, too, and it sickened her to think of handing them over to him.

Or to anyone else for that matter.

"Don't borrow trouble by trying to get the truth out of Darren," he warned her. "I'll ask the questions, and if things get too tense, I want you back in the truck." He waited until she nodded before walking with her toward the house.

And toward Darren.

She instantly spotted him. Looking more like a model on a glossy magazine cover than a real cowboy, he was pacing the porch that wrapped around the house. His gaze snapped in their direction as they approached. His ink-black hair was as fashionably disheveled as his jeans and shirt, and she knew he'd had them custom-made.

Darren wasn't alone. There were two men in suits milling around him.

"You know them?" Tucker whispered to her.

"No, but they look like lawyers."

The one on the right did, anyway. He was on the phone having a whispered conversation. The other eased his hand inside his jacket as they approached. He quit easing when Tucker tapped the badge pinned to his shirt and slid his hand over his own weapon.

Laine's attention went to the ME crew on the left side of that massive porch. There, amid some flame-red rosebushes, she spotted the woman's arm. It flung out at an unnatural angle.

Laine went closer. And saw the face. Bloodless.

Now.

The rain had washed her clean and left her bone-white. Her eyes were open and fixed in a permanently blank stare. Laine's thoughts jerked back to those moments in the parking lot. The sound of the bullets being fired. The image of her body being dragged into the car.

"It's the same woman those men shot," Laine managed to say to Tucker. "You're sure it's Dawn?"

"Yeah." Tucker drew in a long breath and maneuvered Laine away from the body. He positioned himself partially in front of her when he faced Darren.

Darren stopped pacing. "Tucker," he greeted. "Laine."

She kept her own greeting at a nod. Best not to trust her voice right now. She no longer loved Darren, hadn't in a long time, but any emotion that came through wouldn't be good.

Mercy, was she looking at a killer?

"I didn't do this," Darren volunteered. "I *wouldn't* do this," he amended.

"Then how'd her body get here?" Tucker asked.

"How the hell should I know?" He groaned, scrubbed his hand over his face. "I just know I didn't put her there."

"Someone did," Tucker snapped. "You didn't hear anyone or see anything?"

"No, and if I had, I would have called the cops." He cursed and started pacing again. "I'm not stupid. If I'd killed someone, do you really think I'd use my own rose bed as a body dump?"

Tucker glanced around, and Laine followed his gaze. No security cameras were visible, but the private road leading to the place was at least a quarter of a mile long. It would have been awfully brassy of the gunmen to bring her body here, but then they'd already shown a brassy streak by attacking Dawn, and then Tucker and Laine, in broad daylight.

Tucker lifted his shoulder. "You might have dumped her body here if you thought it'd take suspicion off yourself."

That brought on a new round of profanity, and one of the suited men on the porch tried to pull Darren aside. Probably to tell him to say nothing else. But Darren only threw off the man's grip and came down the steps. Tucker adjusted, keeping himself in front of her.

"I don't need to take suspicion off myself," Darren said, his teeth coming together. "Because I didn't do this." He glanced at the body, and the color blanched from his face, making the dark stubble seem even darker.

If her ex was guilty, he was certainly putting up a convincing act of being innocent.

"I need you to come in for questioning," Tucker said, using his Ranger's voice now. It wasn't a suggestion. "You can follow my brother to the Sweetwater Springs sheriff's office." He motioned toward Colt, who was next to the body.

Darren just stared at Tucker. "And if I refuse?"

"You won't, because if you're really innocent as you say you are, you'll want to help us catch whoever did this to Dawn."

The staring contest went on for several moments, and Darren finally nodded. "I do want to catch this SOB. And I want to know what happened to the baby Dawn was carrying."

Laine nearly blurted out the question that was on her mind. Were the babies his? But Tucker had already told her to stay quiet. Tucker stayed quiet, too, but he aimed a very intense glare at Darren.

"I have a right to know," Darren insisted. "Because the baby's mine."

"You're sure?" Tucker asked.

"Positive. Dawn told me she was carrying my child, and then she disappeared."

"Maybe Dawn lied," Laine said, and she got a dose of Tucker's glare. Darren's, too. This wasn't exactly a neutral subject for her, so she matched their glares.

"Dawn didn't lie," Darren fired back. "And that means I have a right to the child."

Tucker shook his head. "I'm guessing Dawn wasn't your usual type of woman. I'm also guessing you knew she had a record."

"Yeah, and she was a criminal informant or something."

"She told you that?" Tucker snapped.

"In a roundabout way." Darren paused, and Laine could see the muscles tighten in his body. "What did Dawn have, a boy or a girl?"

Even now, that was important. Maybe more than the dead woman lying just yards away. There was only one person Laine knew who wanted a child more than she did.

Darren.

And he just might have gotten his wish.

It wasn't out of pettiness that she hesitated, even though Darren was perhaps getting the very thing she'd longed for. This was about the babies' safety. She wouldn't have wanted to hand them over to anyone unless she knew they would be safe from danger.

Tucker paused a moment, too. "Just how much did Dawn tell you about the pregnancy?"

That improved Darren's posture. His shoulders snapped back. "That the kid was mine. She was five months pregnant last time I saw her."

"And you didn't think to report to the police that she was missing?"

"I didn't know she was missing!" he practically shouted. Again, one of the suits tried to pull him back, but Darren threw off his grip with far more force than was necessary. The force of a man who was used to getting his way. "Dawn and I had an argument, all right? She left."

"What'd you argue about?" Tucker pressed.

There it was again. That flash of anger in Darren's dust-gray eyes. "A few of my friends had insulted her. Had called her a gold digger. She wanted me to prove my feelings for her by marrying her."

Judging from his renewed scowl, Dawn's demand

hadn't gone over well. Darren wasn't the sort of man who would look kindly on blackmail. Or marrying beneath him. He came from old money, his family practically royalty in the county, and she was betting his parents wouldn't have approved of someone like Dawn.

Heck, they'd barely approved of her, and her family had money, too.

"After Dawn left, I looked for her so I could pay her medical expenses, but I didn't find her." Darren walked closer to them. "And now I want to know if I fathered a boy or a girl."

"I'll let you know when and if we get paternity test results. That's something else you can do when you come to the sheriff's office—give a DNA sample for us to compare. The sooner you get down there, the sooner the test can be done."

One of the suits came forward. "My client has said he fathered this child, and you have no proof to the contrary. He should be allowed to see the baby."

"Normally, he would," Tucker agreed, and then tipped his head to what was left of Dawn. "But in this case, your client could be responsible for that dead body over there."

"I don't have a motive for killing Dawn!" Darren snapped.

"She was your former lover. You admit to arguing with her. And she left you. Now she's dead on your property, and you've got more than enough in your bank account to have hired someone to kill her. That's means, motive and opportunity, and I wouldn't be much of a lawman to dismiss it just because you're telling me to."

Darren's gaze slashed to Laine. "You believe this?"

He didn't wait for her to answer. "Or is this your way of getting back at me? Were you that jealous of Dawn?"

"I didn't even know you were involved with her until today." That made it even more ironic that Dawn had escaped the baby farm and come to her.

Or maybe not so ironic at all.

"Did you tell Dawn about me?" Laine asked.

Darren made a dismissive sound. "She knew you and I were once engaged. She saw pictures of us around the house."

Laine and Tucker exchanged glances, and they didn't have to say it aloud to know where this was going. Maybe Dawn hadn't come to Laine because she'd seen her at the baby farm. Maybe she had come to Laine because of her connection to Darren, her babies' father.

Maybe.

"Why wouldn't Dawn have come to you?" Laine asked Darren. She left out the part about Dawn being held captive at the baby farm and her escape. Laine thought she still might learn something.

And she did.

She saw the pain flash through his eyes. She knew Darren well enough to know that this hadn't been some causal relationship. Too much emotion for that. But was the pain for the death of a woman he'd loved, or for the child he couldn't quite claim?

"I guess Dawn couldn't forgive me for not marrying her," Darren said, shaking his head. "That's why she didn't come here."

"Or maybe she was scared of you," Tucker challenged. Darren howled about his innocence again, but Tucker ignored it. "Be at the sheriff's office in one hour. If not, I'll issue a warrant for your arrest."

"Wait," Darren said as they started to walk away. He waited until they'd turned back around before he continued. "You two aren't together, are you?"

Tucker huffed. "Not like you're thinking. Laine's helping with the case."

Heaven forbid, it sounded like a lie.

Felt like one, too.

Darren kept staring at them, and his mouth tightened. "Just make sure she doesn't help you railroad me straight into jail."

"Has Laine got a reason to railroad you?" Tucker asked. "Or was that just a dig for the sake of slamming an old flame?"

Darren got another look that she knew too well. Cocky, with a mean streak. "She was your old flame, too. At least you had a thing for her when you two were kids. How'd that work out for you?"

"Yeah, it was a slam, just like I thought," Tucker concluded. He tapped his badge again. "One hour. Personally, I'm hoping you'll be late so I can cuff you and haul your butt in."

Maybe because Darren's *slam* had made him ornery, Tucker slipped his arm around her waist. No doubt it was just to get her moving, but Darren wouldn't have missed the little gesture. He probably thought they'd put their differences aside and joined forces against him.

While landing in bed.

Darren had no idea just how much tension there still was between her and Tucker. Tension that would always be there. Except, of course, when there was a different kind of tension from the touching and long looks.

Like now, for instance.

It was all part of the "rile Darren up" act, she assured

herself, but her body kept nudging her to do something more than just look at the man who had her hormonal number.

"You think he had her killed?" Tucker asked.

It took Laine a moment to switch gears and get back to the only thing that should have been on her mind. Finding Dawn's killer. "I don't want to think it could be true. It's easier to believe her death's just connected to the baby farm."

"But Darren could be connected to that, too. A man who wants a baby as badly as he does could have done some desperate things. Maybe when Dawn tried to run away from him, he had her kidnapped and taken to the baby farm until she delivered. If she escaped, he wouldn't have liked that much."

Laine had to process it first, but eventually, she nodded. "It's possible. Darren has a temper, and if he thought Dawn had betrayed him in some way, he could have struck out in anger."

Tucker mumbled some profanity. "And you were going to marry that jerk?"

"Yes." But then she shook her head. "Maybe."

He looked at her as if she'd sprouted wings.

"I wanted a family," she explained. "You know, mom, dad, babies. He wanted the same thing."

Yet another sprouted-wings look. "What about love?"

Here was where things got a little tricky. "I'd just turned thirty, and I thought time was running out for having that family. And Darren was there, pushing for the very life that I desperately wanted. For a while I thought that was enough."

Tucker mumbled some profanity, shook his head. "My advice—never settle for *enough*."

Laine nearly smiled at Tucker giving relationship advice, but she didn't have a chance to respond because his phone rang. They got into the truck before he took it from his pocket and looked at the screen.

"It's Rosalie," he said.

That put Laine on instant alert. "The babies," she managed to say.

All sorts of bad things started running through her head. Obviously through Tucker's, too, because he fumbled with the phone, trying to answer it quickly.

"Tucker, you need to get back here right away," Rosalie said the moment she came on the line. "Martin Hague's here with a court order, and he's taking the babies."

Chapter Nine

Thank God the roads were no longer wet, because Tucker knew he was driving way too fast. Everything inside him was racing, too, and even though he'd sworn to uphold the law, there was no way he was going to let Hague use that court order to take the babies.

The trouble was, he didn't know exactly how to stop him.

It was hardly legal extenuating circumstances for Tucker to say he wouldn't hand over the babies because he didn't trust the social worker.

But he didn't.

And it wasn't just all that unexplained money that Reed had uncovered, or the fact that one of the women rescued from the baby farm was Hague's cousin. It was something else.

Something that Tucker couldn't quite put his finger on.

He'd already called Hague's boss, Rita Longley, as soon as he'd left Darren's ranch, and Tucker had told the woman to back off on the court order. He hadn't out-right accused Hague of wrongdoing, but he'd warned Ms. Longley that Hague could have a conflict of interest and that he should be pulled from this particular case.

Tucker hadn't gotten a resounding yes from Hague's

boss, so she might not agree with Tucker's demand. But even if she did, it might not be soon enough to stop what Hague had already set into motion.

"Hurry," Laine repeated.

She was obviously just as distressed about this as he was, maybe more. Tucker hoped like the devil that all their concern was for the babies' safety and not for the babies themselves.

There was a difference.

And it wasn't a good thing for a lawman to lose his objectivity, especially when the babies could belong to a man—Darren—who was just as desperate to get his hands on them as Hague apparently was.

Tucker turned onto the ranch road and immediately spotted Hague's car parked directly in front of the house. Like his other visit, he had a Department of Public Safety officer with him, and the guy was on the steps, along with Hague, Rosalie and Mary. The women each had a baby in their arms, and it was clear from their body language that there was a full-blown argument going on.

The moment Tucker brought his truck to a stop, Laine and he barreled out and headed for the porch.

"You're not taking them," Tucker insisted. "I still don't have the DNA results back yet."

"Then they'll be in foster care while we're waiting for those results," Hague argued. He reached for the baby that Rosalie was holding, and she darted away from him. She no longer had a sweet smile on her face. She looked like a mama hen protecting her chick.

"Does he have the right to do this?" Rosalie asked Tucker.

Yeah, Hague did. But that didn't mean it was going to happen.

Tucker walked past the DPS officer, sending him a back-off glare. Whether he would was anyone's guess, and since the guy was armed, it was a huge concern. If Hague was dirty, then this guy could be, too, and Tucker didn't want any more shots fired.

Laine hurried onto the porch, putting herself between Hague and the others. A maneuver that Hague obviously didn't like, because his cheeks turned to flames.

"I don't understand why you won't let me do my job," Hague argued.

"Because you're a suspect in a murder investigation," Tucker informed him.

Clearly, Hague hadn't been expecting that little bombshell, because he stopped reaching for the baby and snapped toward Tucker. "I have no idea what you're talking about." His eyes widened. "You don't think I had anything to do with their mother's death."

"Did you?" Tucker fired back.

"Absolutely not, and I can't imagine why you'd think there was a connection between Dawn Cowen and me."

"The connection's there. Both your cousin Rhonda and Dawn were held captive at makeshift prisons where their babies would have been sold. Those baby farms were likely run by the same person, or were at least connected to each other."

Hague blinked as if he was hearing this for the first time. And maybe he was, but Tucker wasn't about to take anything he said or did at face value. Not after the attack on Laine and the babies.

"You know where Rhonda is?" Hague asked. "She's been in touch with you?"

Tucker had to shake his head to both, but now he was

the one who was confused. He wasn't faking it, either. "Rhonda's missing again?"

Hague nodded, then sighed. "She's always been a troubled girl. Always disappearing and then showing up when she needs money."

That had made her a prime candidate for the baby farm. No one was out looking for her, and no one would alert the authorities that she was missing. This time there was a reason to send up the red flag.

"Are you telling me you honestly don't know where she is?" Tucker demanded.

"I have no idea. I haven't seen her in weeks."

Hell. Weeks. Tucker wasn't sure who groaned louder, him or Laine.

"Did it occur to you that someone from the baby farm could have kidnapped her again?" Laine asked.

There was no sign that he was the least bit concerned about that. "Why would they take her again? She's not pregnant. She gave birth to a baby less than four months ago and then gave him up for adoption. There's no reason for her to be kidnapped."

Tucker's hands moved to his hips. "Maybe the kidnappers consider her a loose end and want her dead. Maybe *you* consider her a loose end."

That put some venom back in his eyes. "There you go again, accusing me of assorted felonies. Well, I'm not guilty of anything other than trying to do my job."

"Then explain your bank account," Tucker fired back. "Explain where you got the cash to buy a house and pay off your student loans."

He pulled back his shoulders. "You've been sticking your nose where it doesn't belong."

"Yeah, I tend to do that when I'm looking for the truth."

Tucker leaned in, violating the guy's personal space and then some. "Like now. Maybe you're as pure as a saint, but if you're not, it wouldn't be wise of me to hand over those newborns to you. You might just turn around and sell them on the black market."

"I wouldn't do that!" Hague's voice was so loud it caused the babies to jump. Even more reason for Tucker to get this guy off the porch.

"Then explain your bank account," Tucker countered.

"I'll explain nothing to you—" Hague was cut off when his phone rang. Tucker was still close enough to see Rita Longley's name appear on the screen. He hoped Hague's boss was reining him in and not giving him the green light to take the babies.

Hague went to the other side of the porch to take the call. Tucker couldn't hear what he was saying, but he used the time to regroup. "Go ahead and take the babies back into the house," Tucker told Mary and Rosalie.

Both women eagerly nodded, and even though Hague shot them a glare, he didn't stop them. He just continued his whispered conversation with his boss. However, the DPS guy looked ready to intervene.

"There's an escaped gunman on the loose," Tucker reminded the lawman. "It's not safe for the newborns to be out here. Not safe for you, either," he added to Laine.

She only shook her head, not budging, so Tucker moved between her and the road just in case the gunman was stupid enough to make a repeat appearance.

"What do we do now?" Laine whispered.

Only then did Tucker realize just how shaky she was. It'd been a bad morning, what with seeing Dawn's body and then this. Sadly, Tucker couldn't even assure her the worst was over.

"We wait and keep investigating," he answered. "But I'd rather you do your waiting inside."

She followed his gaze to the road. No one was there other than some ranch hands milling around, but someone could easily come driving up.

Someone like the killer.

If that person wasn't already on the porch with them. Either way, Tucker wanted her inside. She nodded, obviously ready to do that, but then she stopped when his phone rang. Colt again.

"I'll bet you're ready for some good news," Colt said, and the moment Tucker heard that, he put it on speaker so Laine could hear, too. Yeah, he was ready for something good. "Gene Buford, the gunman we have in custody at the jail, says he's ready to make a plea deal."

"What kind of plea deal?" Tucker asked.

"Says he'll give us information about Dawn in exchange for immunity and placement in witness protection."

"About Dawn and not the person who set all of this up?"

"Just Dawn," Colt answered. "Anything you don't know about her yet?"

"Probably. But this guy tried to kill us," Tucker mumbled. So, he wasn't sure he wanted the guy to walk, no matter what kind of info he provided. Still, he wanted to hear what the idiot had to say.

"How soon can you have him brought over from the jail?" Tucker asked.

"Soon. I can call there now."

Good. The jail was just up the block from the sheriff's office, but it still would take some time to arrange for a guard to have Buford brought over for questioning. The sheriff's office did have a holding cell in case the timing didn't work out so that Tucker could speak to him right away. If necessary, Tucker could go to the jail, but he preferred to do this at the sheriff's office so he could kill two birds with one stone.

"I'll talk to the gunman when I come in to interview Darren," Tucker told Reed. "See you in about a half hour if I can get things settled here that fast."

Tucker ended the call to see how things were about to play out with Hague, but he, too, had finished his call and was glaring at Tucker again. He slammed his phone shut and jammed it back into his pocket.

"Go inside," Tucker whispered to Laine. "Check on the babies."

That got her moving. Good thing, too, because Tucker thought this situation with Hague might turn even uglier than it already was.

"A plea deal, huh?" Hague made a sound that could have meant anything. "Maybe that means this situation with Dawn will be over soon."

"Maybe." And Tucker left it at that. He wasn't exactly pleased that Hague had overheard that conversation, but something like that wouldn't stay a secret for long, especially since the district attorney would have to be brought into any plea-deal talk.

"My supervisor wants to talk to me," Hague grumbled a moment later. "So help me, you'd better not have done anything to compromise my job."

"And you'd better not have done anything to compromise those newborns' safety."

Hague's mouth tightened, and he started down the steps. "I'll try to find Rhonda, and I'll tell her to get in touch with you so you can hear it from her own lips that I had nothing to do with her kidnapping or the baby farms."

"You said you didn't know where she was," Tucker reminded him.

He threw open the door and looked at Tucker from over the roof of the car. "I don't, but I can call some of her friends on the drive back to my office. When you've heard from her, I want you to back off. I'm not the only one with a conflict of interest here, Sergeant McKinnon."

Since Tucker already knew that, and since he was more than thankful just to put an end to this—even a temporary one—he turned and went inside. Laine was waiting for him by the door, and he wasn't sure who made the first move or even how it happened, but she ended up in his arms.

Strange that this kept happening, although it shouldn't have. Even a hug of comfort was a Texas-sized reminder that Laine was the one in his arms. Nothing good could come of this.

Well, nothing reasonable anyway.

Maybe it was because every inch of him was on edge that he even thought of holding her for stress relief. Yeah, for a second or two, it was relief, but what always followed were some crystal clear reminders of why they shouldn't be doing it in the first place.

The heat between them.

The bad blood, too. Hard to hang on to bad blood, though, when the blasted attraction kept getting in the way.

"What are you thinking?" she asked, her breath and body still trembling.

Definitely something he'd keep to himself. Tucker went with the topic that should be on his mind.

"If I'm wrong about Hague, I'll apologize," Tucker mumbled. He truly hoped he was wrong about the social worker.

He was already battling a major suspect, Darren, without adding Hague to the mix. Especially since Hague could eventually get his hands on the newborns. Not by kidnapping them, either, but with that dang court order. Of course, Darren could take them, too, if it turned out he was the father. Still, it would be hard to claim his babies if he was sitting in a jail cell for killing their mother.

"You need to get ready for your meeting with Darren," she reminded him, easing away.

He nodded. Didn't move. Hated that he felt the loss of her body heat.

Really?

He had to deal with this now. It wasn't as if he didn't have anything to do other than stand there and mentally whine about her body heat. Or her scent. Or the stupidity of wanting her right back in his arms again.

"Where are the babies?" he asked. Yet another subject he should be dwelling on.

She fluttered her fingers toward the stairs. "Rosalie and Mary put them in the crib. They'd just had their bottles before Hague got here, and according to Rosalie, newborns usually sleep after they eat."

"Not much different from the rest of their day, then. They sleep all the time. Well, except at night."

The corner of her mouth lifted. "Fatherhood not suiting you much?"

Tucker found himself frowning before he even realized he was going to do it. "I get that a lot. I'm not sure it's all warranted."

"Really?" Laine said, with far more surprise than was necessary. "You're a player."

Again he frowned and started for the downstairs office he'd been using. Laine followed right behind him. "I'm not a player. I'm just not interested in anything long-term."

She chuckled. "Which more or less qualifies you as a player."

He shrugged, wrestling with another frown. "Haven't heard of you trying to settle down with any one particular guy since you split with Darren."

Of course, he hadn't heard of her sleeping around, either, which was essentially what she'd just accused him of doing.

Tucker couldn't deny it, so he shut up and hoped she'd move on to a different subject.

"I've hit a nerve," she said. "I'm sorry."

So much for her moving on. So much for him shutting up, too. He just kept blathering. "I doubt that. Well, you may be sorry that I'm giving you the stink eye, but I doubt you're sorry you brought it up. I know you don't approve of my lifestyle."

"It's not that." She hesitated, shook her head, mumbled something he didn't catch. "How many real kisses have you had?"

"Excuse me?" Tucker felt another frown coming on. Possibly more blathering, too.

"A real kiss," she repeated. "And I don't mean those *unzip me* kisses with your conquests from the Outlaw Bar. I mean real honest-to-goodness kisses that you feel in more than just one part of your body?"

Okay, so Laine had moved on from semisafe conversation about relationships to this. Whatever *this* was. Well, if she wanted to hold a mirror up to his face, she was about to get one turned right back on her.

"How many?" Tucker repeated. "Two. One was with you right there in the kitchen at my granddaddy's house. Yeah, we were just kids, but trust me, it was real."

She swallowed hard, and her forehead bunched up. "And the second kiss?"

"This one." Before he could talk himself out of it, Tucker slid his hand around the back of Laine's neck, hauled her to him and did the one thing he was pretty sure he shouldn't do.

He kissed her.

For real.

There it was. The slam of her body heat and taste all at once. Yeah, he remembered it from all those years before, but it was even better now. Of course it was, because if it hadn't been, Tucker might have stood a chance of giving this particular mistake a fast ending. As it was, fast didn't even appear to be an option. Not to his fired-up body, anyway.

He dragged her closer and made things even worse by deepening the kiss. That taste set him on fire, and the rest of her didn't help cool him down, either. Probably because Laine did some dragging of her own, pulling him closer and closer until they were plastered against each other. He could feel parts of her that he had no right to feel.

But he did, anyway.

Her breasts against his chest. Her sex close to his. Her taste, her breath. Everything.

It was too much to feel all at once. Too much to stop, too, with parts of him already begging for more. Much more. Like them naked on a bed. That's why he was a little surprised when Laine managed to stop.

She stepped back again, her gaze meeting his, and he saw the same *What the heck did we just do?* expression on her face that was no doubt on his. So much for holding up a bloomin' mirror to her face.

Now he'd be lucky if he could walk.

"How bad are you regretting that?" she asked, sliding her tongue over her bottom lip. That simple gesture caused his body to clench and beg for more.

"As much as you are," Tucker settled for saying.

She shook her head, pushed her hair from her face. "Good."

But she didn't clarify what that *good* meant. Nor did she move too far from him. "Remind me not to play a dangerous game like that with you again."

Right. Maybe he should tell the sun not to rise, too. He might have better success there. "You think a reminder will fix this?"

"This?" she questioned.

The heat. The need. And even the little niggling feeling that it had been more than a blasted kiss. Which it couldn't have been, so he darn sure wasn't about to describe it to her. "I'll explain it if you'll explain your *good*."

Though he had a pretty solid idea of that *good,* too. Like him, Laine wanted one of them to stay sane during all this close-quarters stuff.

Best of luck with that.

Laine immediately backed up. Smart woman. They were indeed playing a dangerous game, and Tucker couldn't be certain they both wouldn't play another round the next time their guards were down.

His phone rang, yanking him back to his senses. Not exactly where he wanted to be at first, but seeing the name on the screen, he mentally adjusted.

"It's Rhonda Wesson," he told Laine.

He doubted this was a coincidence. Doubted, too, that Hague hadn't known exactly where she was, because obviously he'd managed to get in touch with his cousin shortly after driving away from the ranch.

"Sergeant McKinnon," she greeted. "My cousin said I should call you."

He waited for her to verify that Hague was innocent and had nothing to do with the baby farms.

She didn't do that.

"Are you all right?" Tucker asked.

Rhonda didn't say anything for several seconds. "No. I need to talk to you. I need help."

"What's wrong?" he couldn't ask fast enough.

"I'm in hiding," Rhonda answered. "Because someone's trying to kill me."

Chapter Ten

Laine watched through the observation glass as Tucker finished up his interview with Darren. Her ex hadn't said anything remotely incriminating and had instead stuck to his broken record claim that he was innocent in Dawn's death.

And maybe he was.

Still, Laine was glad that Tucker was being thorough with this interview. If he cleared Darren as a suspect, and the DNA results came back proving the babies were his, then Darren would walk away with them as fast as he could. He'd be doing it legally, too.

Hide them. Protect them, Dawn had said to Laine just seconds before those men had gunned her down, and Laine intended to do everything she could to carry out the woman's dying request.

It was odd that Tucker had taken on the same mission. Not just the investigation. He wouldn't have let go of that. But he also didn't seem ready to let go of the babies. He was definitely not the old Tucker.

Well, at least not in that way.

The kiss had certainly been evidence of the charmer cowboy who'd coaxed plenty of women into his bed. Laine had to be careful that the same didn't happen to her. The last thing she needed was to be another notch on his rodeo belt.

Even if that kiss had made her think differently.

For a few heated moments anyway, it'd caused her common sense to take a serious nosedive. Best to avoid future kissing so she could keep a clear head. Too bad just a mental warning wouldn't be enough.

Not even close.

She had to figure out a way to put some physical distance between her and Tucker. Without sacrificing the safety of the babies, of course.

She and Tucker had left them at the ranch with Colt, his father, Rayanne, Rosalie and Mary. In addition, Tucker had put some of the ranch hands on alert. They weren't trained guards by any means, but they were all armed. Hopefully their presence would prevent the missing attacker from trying to get on the grounds.

Maybe Tucker and she would get some other help with that, too.

Just up the hall in one of the other interview rooms, the gunman that'd already been arrested, Gene Buford, was waiting with his lawyer to talk to Tucker about a possible plea deal in exchange for information about Dawn.

"Are we finally finished here?" Darren said, his voice stern enough to snap Laine's attention back to the interview.

"For now." Tucker stood when Darren did, and they faced each other across a gray metal table. "I'll let you know about the GSR test."

Darren mumbled something she didn't catch and scowled, clearly not happy. Tucker had swabbed Darren's hands for gunshot residue—something that could have perhaps linked him to Dawn's shooting.

GSR alone wouldn't be enough to charge him, since Darren could always say he'd fired a gun elsewhere. It wasn't that unusual for a rancher to have to shoot a rattler or some other predatory animal that'd strayed onto the property. But the GSR might cast enough suspicion that Tucker could get a court order to examine Darren's bank account and maybe get a search warrant for his house.

Darren and Tucker were still in a glaring match when Reed appeared in the doorway of the observation room.

"Rhonda Wesson just arrived," Reed told her.

Laine stepped out, not sure she would even recognize the woman. She hadn't been part of the rescue of the women and babies from the farm where Rhonda had been held, but there had been some photos of her in the news. Laine remembered a scraggly looking pregnant woman dressed in green scrubs.

Which was very unlike the woman she saw now.

It took Laine a moment to connect the tall blonde to that rescued woman.

Definitely no scrubs today. Rhonda was wearing dress pants and a white top. Not a strand of her hair was out of place. She seemed more suited to being in a boardroom than to being in hiding, but there was concern in her cool green eyes as they swept around the sheriff's office and landed on Laine.

"You must be Dr. Braddock," Rhonda said, coming toward her with her hand extended. From the looks of it, she'd recently had a manicure.

"Call me Laine." She shook hands with her, and even though Rhonda held eye contact for several seconds, her attention drifted to the closed doors of the interview rooms.

"Excuse me," Rhonda said when she noticed that

Laine's gaze had followed hers. "Police stations make me nervous. Actually, being anywhere in public right now makes me feel that way. I don't want to stay long. I just want to talk to you and Sergeant McKinnon."

Laine was about to assure her that would happen just as one of the interview room doors opened, and Tucker stepped out. Darren and his lawyer were right behind him.

"You need to get off this witch hunt," Darren snapped, looking at Laine, and then at Rhonda. He barely spared her a glance.

Rhonda had a much stronger reaction.

She stepped behind Tucker, her attention fixed on Darren. "I didn't know he'd be here."

"I was interviewing him," Tucker explained.

"Railroading me," Darren corrected. "Is that why you're here, Rhonda? You planning to railroad me, too?"

"You know each other?" Tucker asked.

"Know her? She tried to milk money from me just a few weeks ago."

"I didn't," Rhonda insisted. "I just wanted to talk to you about Dawn, and I wanted to see if you were the person following me." She paused, swallowed hard. "Dawn was terrified of you."

"She wasn't, and you're saying that just because you're riled that I wouldn't pay you off."

Frantically shaking her head, Rhonda turning to Tucker. "We need to talk, but not with him around."

Rhonda threw open the door to the other interview room. Gene Buford was cuffed at his hands and feet, and he was seated with his court-appointed attorney. Both turned in Rhonda's direction, as did the guard who'd brought Buford over from the jail.

The moment seemed to freeze. Gene Buford was in

YOUR PARTICIPATION IS REQUESTED!

Dear Reader,

Since you are a lover of our books – we would like to get to know you!

Inside you will find a short Reader's Survey. Sharing your answers with us will help our editorial staff understand who you are and what activities you enjoy.

To thank you for your participation, we would like to send you 2 books and 2 gifts – **ABSOLUTELY FREE!**

Enjoy your gifts with our appreciation,

Pam Powers

SEE INSIDE FOR READER'S SURVEY

For Your Reading Pleasure...

YOUR READER'S SURVEY
"THANK YOU" FREE GIFTS INCLUDE:
▶ 2 FREE books
▶ 2 lovely surprise gifts

PLEASE FILL IN THE CIRCLES COMPLETELY TO RESPOND

1) What type of fiction books do you enjoy reading? (Check all that apply)
- ○ Suspense/Thrillers ○ Action/Adventure ○ Modern-day Romances
- ○ Historical Romance ○ Humour ○ Paranormal Romance

2) What attracted you most to the last fiction book you purchased on impulse?
- ○ The Title ○ The Cover ○ The Author ○ The Story

3) What is usually the greatest influencer when you <u>plan</u> to buy a book?
- ○ Advertising ○ Referral ○ Book Review

4) How often do you access the internet?
- ○ Daily ○ Weekly ○ Monthly ○ Rarely or never

5) How many NEW paperback fiction novels have you purchased in the past 3 months?
- ○ 0 - 2 ○ 3 - 6 ○ 7 or more

YES! I have completed the Reader's Survey. Please send me the 2 FREE books and 2 FREE gifts (gifts are worth about $10) for which I qualify. I understand that I am under no obligation to purchase any books, as explained on the back of this card.

❑ **I prefer the regular-print edition**
182/382 HDL GF94

❑ **I prefer the larger-print edition**
199/399 HDL GF94

FIRST NAME	LAST NAME

ADDRESS

APT.#	CITY

STATE/PROV.	ZIP/POSTAL CODE

EMAIL

Accepting your 2 free Harlequin Intrigue® books and 2 free gifts (gifts valued at approximately $10.00) places you under no obligation to buy anything. You may keep the books and gifts and return the shipping statement marked "cancel." If you do not cancel, about a month later we'll send you 6 additional books and bill you just $4.74 each for the regular-print edition or $5.49 each for the larger-print edition in the U.S. or $5.24 each for the regular-print edition or $5.99 each for the larger-print edition in Canada. That is a savings of at least 13% off the cover price. It's quite a bargain! Shipping and handling is just 50¢ per book in the U.S. and 75¢ per book in Canada.* You may cancel at any time, but if you choose to continue, every month we'll send you 6 more books, which you may either purchase at the discount price or return to us and cancel your subscription. *Terms and prices subject to change without notice. Prices do not include applicable taxes. Sales tax applicable in N.Y. Canadian residents will be charged applicable taxes. Offer not valid in Quebec. Books received may not be as shown. All orders subject to credit approval. Credit or debit balances in a customer's account(s) may be offset by any other outstanding balance owed by or to the customer. Please allow 4 to 6 weeks for delivery. Offer available while quantities last.

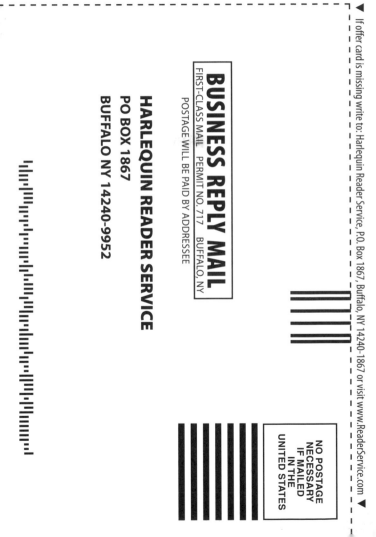

BUSINESS REPLY MAIL
FIRST-CLASS MAIL   PERMIT NO. 717   BUFFALO, NY

POSTAGE WILL BE PAID BY ADDRESSEE

HARLEQUIN READER SERVICE
PO BOX 1867
BUFFALO NY 14240-9952

NO POSTAGE
NECESSARY
IF MAILED
IN THE
UNITED STATES

◀ If offer card is missing write to: Harlequin Reader Service, P.O. Box 1867, Buffalo, NY 14240-1867 or visit www.ReaderService.com ▶

the process of getting to his feet when he looked into the hall where Laine, Tucker, Rhonda, Darren and his lawyer were standing.

Buford eased back into his chair.

"We've waited long enough," Buford's attorney snapped. She was a petite brunette who looked as if she'd just finished law school. Hardly the voice of authority.

"And you'll wait some more," Tucker snarled back, shutting the door. He tossed Darren one of his hard glares, and both Darren and his lawyer finally left.

"Sorry," Rhonda mumbled. "I'm just shaken up."

"Because of Darren Carty?" Tucker asked.

She nodded. Then shook her head. Her fingers were trembling when she brushed her hair from her cheek. "It's not a good idea for me to be here."

"You're safe," Tucker assured her, and he led Laine and Rhonda into the empty interview room. "Why are you scared of Darren?"

"My cousin Martin told me that Darren was a suspect in Dawn's murder and that he might be the person who's been following me."

Rhonda sat next to Laine, and the woman turned to her when she continued. "I'm pretty sure someone's been following me, and I think it's connected to Dawn."

"How?" Laine asked. "Why?"

"I'm not positive, but I think it has to do with that black-market baby operation where we were held captive."

Laine was almost certain of that. "How well did you know Dawn?" Laine pressed.

Rhonda drew in another shivery breath. "We were held together for a while. Until they moved her to another place. That's around the time Sergeant McKinnon here rescued me." She paused, looking up at him. "I can never thank you enough for that."

Tucker nodded. "We hope you can help us find Dawn's killer."

"You mean it isn't Darren?"

"It could be, but we're looking into several possibilities." Tucker didn't mention that her cousin was one of those suspects. "Tell us what's been happening since you were rescued."

Rhonda put her hand on her stomach. "Well, obviously I had my baby. A boy that I gave up for adoption. I can barely manage to take care of myself, much less a baby."

Laine couldn't argue with that. She'd read through the woman's bio on the drive to the sheriff's office, and even though she was in her early thirties, Rhonda had never held a real job for more than a few months. She was smart, though, and had managed to finish a college degree while serving time for embezzlement and extortion. She'd been out of jail for six years now and in that time had stayed clean and off the radar.

Well, until she'd been taken captive and then rescued at the baby farm.

Of course, Rhonda looked as if she had gotten past her shady roots. At least when it came to her appearance.

"Dawn talked about Darren while you were both being held captive?" Tucker continued.

Rhonda nodded. "She was scared of him and even hinted that he might be the reason she was there. Dawn had tried to get away from him, you see. He didn't really want her, only the baby, and after they had an argument, she told him she didn't want him to raise the child. She'd planned to give it to someone else, someone who'd be a good father."

That meshed with some of the other things they'd learned, but Laine still had a hard time imagining Darren kidnapping his pregnant girlfriend to keep her from giving up his baby. Of course, she also understood this need to be a parent and have a family. Maybe Darren had just taken that need too far.

Rhonda twisted a plain gold ring on her thumb. "What about the baby? Wait, I remember right before Dawn was moved, she found out she was carrying twins." She leaned closer to Tucker. "Are they here? God, please tell me Darren can't get his hands on them."

"No, they've been moved to a safe house," Tucker said.

A lie, of sorts, since the babies were actually at the ranch, but Laine was glad he wasn't giving out their whereabouts. Especially to this woman, who unnerved her. Maybe it was the perfect clothes and manicure, but something about Rhonda didn't feel right.

"Good." Rhonda repeated it as she eased back deeper into her chair. "Dawn would have wanted them kept out of harm's way. Did either of you get a chance to see Dawn before she was killed?"

Tucker shook his head, and Rhonda turned to Laine, obviously waiting for an answer.

"I didn't know her," Laine settled for saying.

"Really? Because I'd heard you were involved with the baby farm investigation."

"I was, uh, removed from the case."

"Oh." Rhonda cast an uneasy glance at Tucker, who thankfully didn't elaborate.

"Tell me about your cousin Martin Hague," Tucker went on. "Any chance he was involved with the baby farm?"

Rhonda's eyes widened, and it seemed to take her a moment to realize Tucker was being serious. "Why?"

"Because he's shown a lot of interest in Dawn's babies, that's why."

Rhonda just shook her head again. She looked to be on the verge of dismissing any possibility of her cousin's guilt. Then she blew out a long, frustrated breath. "Maybe."

That got Tucker and Laine's complete attention. *"Maybe?"* Tucker pressed.

"Martin's always been ambitious. Always looking for an angle to make money."

"Then why'd he become a social worker?" Laine asked.

"I think it was because of the adoption opportunities. There's a lot more money in that than people think, and the job would give him contact with women he could coax into giving up their babies.

"You didn't know he'd helped with some adoptions?" Rhonda added when they just stared at her.

"No, and I'd like some details about that," Tucker insisted.

"Well, there won't be records, that's for sure. Martin's too careful for that. He just connects pregnant women with potential buyers…I mean, parents who'll pay for a private adoption."

"And how do you know this?" Laine asked.

"Because that's what he tried to do to me. He found some family that would have paid me twenty grand for my baby. I didn't like them when I met them so I said no. A couple of weeks later, I was kidnapped and taken to that hellhole of a place that the press dubbed the baby farm."

She and Tucker exchanged relieved glances. Finally, this was some fodder to stop Hague and that blasted court order. Maybe. Rhonda had already said there'd be no records, but it was possible to connect the extra money in Hague's bank account to the adoptions of his clients.

Rhonda shook her head again. "I don't think Martin's responsible for my kidnapping. He's greedy, but I don't think he has the grit to do something like that. Besides, he probably thought he could just set up another private adoption for me. That's what he did after I was rescued and had my son."

"Hague helped with that?" Tucker asked.

"Yes. It was a different family from the first one, and I really liked them."

Tucker frowned. "They paid you?"

Rhonda nodded. "I didn't exactly have any extra cash after you rescued me, so yes, I took some money for the private adoption. That money's almost gone now, and I need a safe place to stay."

Well, that money explained the expensive-looking clothes.

Tucker hesitated a moment. "I'll see what arrangements I can make for a safe house. Wait here." He motioned for Laine to follow him. She did, and when they stepped out into the hall, he shut the door.

"I don't trust her," Laine immediately whispered. "Women in hiding from a would-be killer don't usually have time for a manicure."

Tucker made a sound of surprise to indicate it wasn't something he had even considered. "I want to get Rhonda's accusations about Hague on record." He glanced at his watch. "All this might take a while, and I still need to talk to the idiot who wants a plea deal. I can have someone take you back out to the ranch."

It was tempting, but Laine didn't even get a chance to consider it before Tucker's phone rang.

"It's Darren," he relayed to her. "What do you want?" he demanded, putting the call on speaker.

"I need to tell you something that might pertain to Rhonda."

Whatever it was, it obviously wasn't good, because Laine could hear the doom and gloom in Darren's voice.

Tucker glanced at the door and then the screen, and led her to the break room at the end of the hall. Probably because he didn't want Rhonda or the gunman behind door number two listening in on the conversation.

"What about Rhonda?" Tucker prompted Darren once he was sure the chat would be private.

"I just found a message on my voice mail from Dawn. Things have been so hectic around here, and I just got around to checking it."

Tucker jumped right on that. "When did she call?"

"Yesterday. She sounded terrified and wanted me to come pick her up. She said she was in Sweetwater Springs. Is that where she was killed?"

"You said this was possibly about Rhonda," Tucker reminded him.

"Yeah." Darren sounded more than a little irritated, maybe because Tucker hadn't answered his question. "It's a bit hard to understand what Dawn is saying, but it sounds as if she says 'I'm running from her. I thought I could trust her, but I can't.'"

Tucker huffed. "And why would you think that meant Rhonda?"

"Because why else would she have lied and said Dawn was afraid of me? She wasn't. And the only reason Rhonda would have lied would have been to make you suspicious of someone other than herself. She's a suspect, right?"

"I'm not sure what she is," Tucker admitted. "But I do want a recording of that message. Send it to me here at the sheriff's office so I can get it to the Ranger lab for analysis."

"I will, but so help me, McKinnon, you'd better not try to use this against me in some way."

"You got something to hide?" Tucker was already talking to the air, because Darren had hung up.

Tucker looked at her, and she could practically see the wheels turning in his head. "Her manicure means something, huh?" he mumbled.

"I'd like more proof than that, too," Laine countered, "but maybe it's a start." She paused. "Unless Dawn was talking about me when she said she thought she could trust *her*."

"You?" he challenged. "She came to you for help."

"Maybe. Or maybe she got to my office and thought I'd betrayed her or something. Maybe she even thought that I was the one who sent those killers after her. I could be the *her* in the message she left for Darren."

"She still trusted you enough to ask you to protect her twins." Tucker stayed quiet a moment, then scrubbed his hand over his face. "I need to question Rhonda more about her relationship with Dawn."

Laine agreed, and this time she stayed back, not wanting to compromise what was now an official interrogation of a possible suspect and not just an interview with a possible informant.

Tucker threw open the door of the room where they'd left Rhonda, and he cursed.

The room was empty, and Rhonda was gone.

Chapter Eleven

Well, this day sure as heck wasn't going as Tucker had planned. Rhonda was on the run again, and he was no closer to solving the case than he had been when he'd woken up. Something had to give, and it had to give soon.

"Maybe we can catch up with Rhonda," Laine suggested. "She couldn't have gotten far."

"Not *we*," he instantly corrected. "No way do I want you out there trying to hunt down a suspect."

And since Reed was the only deputy in the sheriff's office, Tucker didn't want him out there, either. He was about to ask Reed to call for someone from the jail to look for Rhonda, but then his phone rang, and he saw the woman's name on the screen.

"Where are you, Rhonda?" Tucker demanded the moment he answered.

"I'm sorry, but I just couldn't stay there. I heard you talking to Darren, and I figured he was setting me up to take the fall for him. Or to be attacked. I don't want to die like Dawn."

Tucker groaned. "No one was going to attack you while you were here."

He hoped. Still, Tucker couldn't rule out the possibility that Rhonda had a legitimate concern. Laine's expression let him know that she felt the same way. Darren had the means necessary to go after anyone who could link him to Dawn's murder, and maybe Laine's ex thought Rhonda fell into that category.

"My offer stands," he added to Rhonda. "I can arrange for you to go to a safe house."

It wasn't a totally selfless offer on his part. Tucker could send her to a place where someone could keep an eye on her if it turned out she'd had some part in the baby farms. A place where he could also keep her alive if she was innocent in all of this.

"I don't want your safe house," she insisted. "I just want to be *safe,* and I'd been doing a good job of that on my own. I hope I didn't make a stupid mistake coming to see you," Rhonda went on, but then she stopped, mumbled some profanity. "I think someone's following me again. I need to go."

Before Tucker could say anything that might stop her, Rhonda hung up. He immediately hit Redial and tried to get her back on the line, but the call went straight to voice mail. She'd no doubt turned off her phone.

Great.

Tucker didn't want to know how long it'd be before he could speak to her and coax her into coming back in for questioning. And besides, maybe it wasn't a good idea bringing her back if someone was truly following her.

Of course, that *if* was just that. An if. Rhonda could be lying through her teeth about everything, especially her lack of involvement in Dawn's murder.

"You still need to talk to Hague," Laine reminded him.

Yeah, because Rhonda's cousin had some things to explain that might shed some light on this case. Or at least some light on Hague himself. Tucker located his number, and the man answered on the first ring.

"I'm on my way there to see Rhonda," Hague said right off the bat. "I'll be at the sheriff's office in about ten minutes, and I'm bringing my lawyer with me."

"Too late. Your cousin's already left. But how the heck did you know she'd be here?"

Hague paused and made a huffing sound, maybe because Tucker hadn't bothered to ask nicely. Tucker wasn't in the mood for stroking egos.

"She called me, all right?" Hague finally answered. "She said she was going to see you, and I thought it'd be my chance to talk to her, to see how she's doing. I also thought she might need a lawyer since she could be involved in something illegal."

Interesting. Especially since Rhonda had her doubts about Hague's innocence. Or maybe she'd just wanted to cast a guilty light on him.

"Illegal, as in the baby farm?" Tucker pressed.

"I don't know. I just know that she's acting even stranger than usual. I figure she's in some kind of trouble. Did she really just leave?" Hague asked, sounding genuinely disappointed. Or else he was doing a good job of faking it.

"She did. She called me right after she left and said someone was following her again. Is it you by any chance?"

"No." Hague stretched that out a few syllables. "And if you're only going to accuse me of more crimes, then this conversation is over."

"It's not over. Not until you explain to me where you got all that extra money in your bank account. Rhonda seems to think it comes from the referral fees that adoptive parents pay you. Is that true?"

It was silent for several long moments. "Rhonda can have a big mouth. She shouldn't have said that."

Maybe not, but Hague wasn't denying it. "Is it true?" Tucker repeated.

"I've done nothing wrong," Hague countered, which was practically code for *Yeah, it's true.*

Now it was Tucker's turn to huff. "I need you back here to give a statement on those funds," he insisted. "Not today, though." One look at Laine's weary eyes, and he figured the last thing she needed was to go another round with Hague. "Be here tomorrow morning, ten o'clock."

"You'll do the interview yourself?" Hague asked.

Normally, a simple question like that wouldn't have put a knot in his gut, but Tucker didn't like the idea of a possible suspect pinning him down to a specific time and place.

It was downright dangerous.

If Hague was guilty, he could use it as an opportunity to attack them again. And even if Tucker left Laine at the ranch for the interview, which he would likely do, it might prompt Hague to go there, knowing that Tucker wouldn't be around to stop him.

"One of the deputies can take your statement," Tucker said. It might or might not have been true.

Tucker hung up, trying to prepare himself to talk with the moron looking for a plea deal, but he needed a moment. Clearly, Laine did, too. Tucker took her back to the break room and poured them each a cup of coffee.

"Uh-oh," Laine mumbled, studying his face. "Are you about to lecture me?"

He was sure he frowned. "A lecture's the last thing on my mind."

Her eyebrows flexed. "Oh."

For a simple little word, it conveyed a lot. So did her gaze, which dropped to his mouth. "Not that, either. I figure it's a good idea if we don't kiss, don't think about kissing and don't even bring up the subject."

The next sound she made was a short *hmm* as she sipped her coffee. "You're right, of course."

It didn't feel or sound right at all.

"Obviously, there's still something between us," he added. "But that kind of something can make a bad situation worse."

An image of her mother flashed through his head. And his family. No one on any side of this mess with Jewell and Whitt Braddock would want to see Laine and him together.

"Maybe that's it," she mumbled. "It's the whole forbidden attraction thing that's drawing us together."

Tucker thought about that a moment. Dismissed it. And because he clearly didn't have much of a brain left, he leaned in and brushed his mouth over hers.

It was nothing—just a touch of their lips. At least it should have been nothing. But as usual with Tucker, things were never simple.

"Nope, nothing to do with anything forbidden," he assured her. "It was there a long time before we ended up on opposite sides."

A knock at the door caused him and Laine to fly apart as if they'd been caught doing something wrong—which they were. It wasn't Rhonda or either of their other suspects. It was the dirtbag's lawyer. The woman was pale, and had beads of sweat above her upper lip.

"I'll be there when I'm ready," Tucker snapped.

"No need. My client's changed his mind. Mr. Buford doesn't want a plea deal after all."

The lawyer would have just darted right out of there if Tucker hadn't snagged her by the arm. "What gives?"

She looked over his shoulder and then shook off Tucker's grip. "I'm not at liberty to say. My client wishes to be returned to his cell now. He's advised me that he intends to remain silent."

Tucker cursed when the lawyer walked away, and he went back through the past half hour to try and figure out what'd gone wrong.

It didn't take him long to come up with something.

"Buford saw Rhonda when she opened the door to the interview room," Tucker said with a groan. "Darren, too. If one of them is his boss, Buford could have seen their presence as some kind of veiled warning for him to keep quiet."

"Well, it worked," Laine said. "What about the one in the hospital? Any chance he'll be willing to make a plea deal?"

"Maybe. But I need to make sure both Darren and Rhonda stay away from him. Hague, too, because Hague could have called Buford's lawyer and told him he was on the way here."

Maybe Buford had thought he could make the deal and be placed in witness protection before his boss learned what was going on. Now something—or more likely, *someone*—had spooked him.

Tucker took out his phone to call the private security company that was guarding the guy, but before he could make the call, his phone rang.

"It's the Ranger crime lab," he relayed to Laine, and he answered it.

"We just got back the results of the babies' DNA tests," the tech said.

Tucker had hoped they'd be back this soon, but he hadn't realized just what an emotional punch it would be when the crime lab called. His stomach tightened again, and when his lungs started to ache he realized he was holding his breath.

"And?" Tucker managed to ask.

"They're fraternal twins, and their mother was indeed the dead woman, Dawn Cowen."

Laine sucked in a lot of air. Not that this was a surprise to her. After all, Dawn had brought the babies to her office, but still it was hard hearing it all spelled out for them.

"And the babies' father?" Tucker asked, though he figured the tech wouldn't have that info. There was no reason for Darren to be in the system, and there wouldn't have been time for his DNA sample to be processed yet.

"It's a man named Kurt Laverty."

Tucker looked at Laine to see if she knew who the man was, but she only shook her head. "You're positive?" he asked the tech.

"Yeah. This is standard paternity test, and it was an easy match since we have Laverty's DNA on file."

There were only a few reasons why the DNA would have been in the system, and knowing Dawn's history, Tucker was betting Laverty wasn't a state or federal employee. It was because he was a criminal.

"Tell me Laverty's in jail," Tucker added, because he didn't want to hand over the babies to some sleazebag who just happened to get Dawn pregnant.

"Oh, he's in jail, all right, and he's been there for the

past four months. He pled out on a double murder charge so he could get the death penalty off the table. He got two consecutive life sentences."

Good. Well, not *good* for the twins. It would have been better if they'd had a decent father who could give them a good life. But at least this way, Laverty wouldn't get his hands on them.

Nor would Darren.

"Now we know," Laine mumbled when Tucker ended the call. She opened her mouth, closed it, then started to pace. "I want to adopt them."

It wasn't exactly a surprise. Tucker had seen her getting attached to the babies, but attachment and motherhood were two different things.

"Dawn could have next of kin who would want them," Tucker reminded her. And if any of Dawn's or Laverty's family members were around, they would have a legal claim.

For that matter, so would family services.

With the results from the DNA test back and the confirmed death of the birth mother, the state could and would take the twins while they sorted it all out.

"Sleep on that," Tucker advised her. Though part of him—an obviously stupid part—hoped she didn't change her mind. Laine would be a good mother.

He didn't have any doubts about that.

Tucker had seen the way she'd handled the babies. He'd also seen how much she'd wanted a child, especially since he now knew she couldn't have one of her own.

"I'd planned on adopting anyway," Laine continued, as Tucker led her out of the break room and toward the front of the building.

"Twins," he reminded her. "They're double the work."

She looked up at him. "Do you really want them to go to strangers?"

"No." Tucker didn't even have to think about that. "I just want what's best for them. And for you."

He groaned, hating that Laine now factored into this. It darn sure didn't help things that he was thinking of what was best for her, rather than what was best overall.

That dang kiss had changed everything.

He stopped by Reed's desk and waited until the deputy had finished a call. "Laine and I are heading out," Tucker told him. "Any word on Dawn's next of kin?"

Reed shook his head. "Her parents are both dead, and she has no siblings. Her mother has a sister, but the Rangers haven't had any luck tracking her down so far."

"Does she have a criminal record?" Laine asked right off the bat.

Another head shake from Reed. "She's a secretary at a bank in San Antonio, but she's on vacation and isn't answering her phone." His eyes widened. "You don't think she's been hurt, do you?"

"No." At least Tucker hoped she hadn't been. "But just in case, have someone from SAPD drop by her place for a welfare check."

Reed nodded, assured him that he would.

So, the babies had an aunt. Maybe one who would want them and crush Laine's dream of adopting them. Tucker hated how this could all turn out, but he especially hated that they had no control over the fate of the newborns they'd been protecting.

"Come on," Tucker said, opening the door.

He glanced around to make sure no one suspicious was lurking in the halls, including Hague, who was still possibly on his way over. Tucker didn't see anyone, so he got Laine moving toward the side parking lot. They were halfway between the sheriff's office and his truck when he spotted movement on the roof just across the street.

But it was too late.

The shot came right at Laine and him.

Chapter Twelve

Laine didn't even have time to react. But Tucker did. He pulled her to the ground.

They landed hard, the concrete scraping against her hands and knees and nearly knocking the breath right out of her. Before Laine could even regain that breath—or think—Tucker had gotten her moving again. He hooked his arm around her, and they rolled to the side of a cruiser.

Barely in time.

Another bullet slammed through the air, landing in the spot where they'd just been.

Cursing, Tucker drew his gun and took aim at the diner across the street. The front of the small building was a wall of windows, and Laine got just a glimpse of the stunned expressions of the diners before Tucker pushed her even farther to the ground.

Sweet heaven. Was the shooter in there with all those people?

If so, not only did Tucker not have a clean shot, but it was also possible he could hit an innocent bystander. At this time of day, there could be families inside.

"You see the shooter?" Reed shouted, and it took her a moment to realize he'd shouted it from an open window in the sheriff's office.

"He's on the roof of the diner," Tucker answered, but then he cursed again when another bullet slammed into the concrete just inches from them.

So the gunman wasn't actually inside, but he could do a lot of damage from the roof. Worse, some of the diners were obviously starting to panic. Laine could hear their screams and shouts for help, and she prayed none of them would run out into the line of fire.

"Call the jail and have them send some guards for backup," Tucker yelled. "Did the guard already leave with Buford?"

"No. Buford's still in the interview room talking with his lawyer."

That obviously didn't please Tucker because he groaned. "Tell them to stay put."

That's when Laine remembered that Reed was the only deputy inside the sheriff's office. Colt was back at the ranch guarding the babies, and Cooper was away on his honeymoon. The night deputies wouldn't be coming in for several hours, and there was no way Tucker would want Buford left alone. It would be too tempting for him to try to escape.

In fact, that might be why this attack was happening. If someone connected with Buford had been watching the sheriff's office, then they would have known this was the perfect time for an attack. A gunman could take out her and Tucker while freeing Buford, and it likely wouldn't matter to this shooter how many innocent people could get caught up in the cross fire.

"Unlock the cruiser," Tucker called out to Reed.

More shots came, and in between the loud blasts, Laine heard the slight clicking sound. A moment later, Tucker threw open the passenger's-side door of the cruiser. Obviously, Reed had managed to unlock it from inside, no doubt using a remote key. The police car wasn't ideal cover because it was parked out in the open, but Laine was thankful for anything that would get her and Tucker out of the path of those bullets.

"Get in and stay down," Tucker told her.

He stayed perched behind the door and in front of her, his gun ready. And with his left hand, he pushed her into the cruiser.

Laine scrambled across the seat, reaching for Tucker to pull him in with her, but he stayed put and adjusted the aim of his gun.

Tucker fired.

The sound was deafening. It was so close that she could have sworn it rattled the windows.

Laine couldn't tell if his shot hit its target, but she guessed it hadn't when the next shot flew into the cruiser's front windshield. The glass was obviously bullet-resistant, but it still cracked and webbed, making it even harder for her to see what was going on.

Tucker levered himself up to fire another shot, but then immediately flattened himself on the ground when a bullet slammed into the cruiser door. The sound of metal ripping through metal caused her heart to pound against her ribs. The door might be bullet-resistant, too, but if the shooter kept it up, the shots could eventually get through, and Tucker could die.

"Get inside the car," she insisted.

Of course, he ignored her and leaned out of the door again.

This time, he didn't even get off a shot before a bullet smacked into his gun. For one heart-stopping moment, Laine thought he'd been hit, and she heard herself call out his name again. The sparks flew, and Tucker dropped his weapon only to snatch it back up again.

"I'm pretty sure this is the moron who tried to kill us at my house," Tucker relayed to her.

It didn't surprise her that he'd come back for them. Laine could still feel his arm around her throat and his gun jammed to her head. He wasn't close enough to do that now, but he could continue to blast his way into the car.

But why?

Why had he or his boss targeted Tucker and her to die?

Laine had gone back to that question over and over, and the only thing she could come up with was Dawn. Maybe the gunman thought Dawn had told her something incriminating. Something that would link back to the person behind not just these attacks but the baby farms themselves. But Dawn had barely managed to say anything before the killers had come for her.

"What the hell's he doing here?" Tucker mumbled.

Laine lifted her head just a fraction and caught a glimpse of Darren across the street. He was in front of the antique store just to the left of the diner. He had his back flat against the store's door, and he, too, had drawn his gun.

Tucker had asked a great question—what was he doing there?

Darren had left the sheriff's office a good half hour before, and while Laine wanted to think that maybe he was still in town just doing errands or something, she didn't like the timing of this.

Was Darren there because he'd hired that shooter on the roof, or was he in the same wrong place/wrong time situation as the diners?

"Get inside the store, Darren!" Tucker shouted to him.

Even over the din of the gunfire, Laine was fairly certain that Darren had heard him, but he ignored Tucker's order and stayed put. Sweet heaven, Tucker didn't need to have that kind of distraction now.

"Two guards are on the way!" Reed shouted out to them.

Good. But they wouldn't be able to get close enough to the shooter without running the risk of being gunned down.

Tucker fired another shot, took out his phone and tossed it to her. "Tell Reed to get those guards at the back of the diner. I want this idiot stopped now."

Laine managed a shaky nod, and with equally shaky hands, she scrolled through the numbers until she located Reed's. The deputy answered on the first ring, and she relayed Tucker's message. Tucker no doubt hadn't wanted to shout it out because he didn't want the guy to have any warning as to what was about to happen.

Maybe he hadn't wanted to alert Darren, either.

"The guards will be at the rear of the diner in just a couple of minutes," Reed confirmed after she heard him make a call. "But we got another problem. That social worker, Hague, and his lawyer just came running into the back of the sheriff's office. He claims he heard the shots and figured this was the safest place to be."

Oh, God. Definitely not good. "He could be there to help Buford escape."

"That's what I figured. I'll keep an eye on him."

That wouldn't be easy because she could still see Reed at the window. He had his gun ready, and his attention was focused on the shooter.

The bullets continued to come at them, but the direction changed a little. Instead of the door, they all seemed to be coming through the windshield. Each one chipped away at the glass and sent her adrenaline soaring.

"Get on the floor," Tucker told her.

He fired some shots at the gunman, reached in the glove compartment, reloaded with a fresh magazine and fired again. Still the bullets kept tearing through the glass, and one finally broke through just as she dropped to the floor. It tore through the car and slammed into the rear windshield.

The shooter might have seen her move, because again the shots shifted and he began to fire into the engine. Where the bullets could eventually reach her. Maybe reach her before the guards got to the diner.

"Do you know how to hot-wire a car?" Tucker asked. Because of the gunshots, he had to yell it.

Laine shook her head.

"Then you're about to learn, because there's no remote starter for the cruiser. Stay on the floor, get that Swiss Army knife in the glove compartment and use it to open the ignition cover." He motioned toward the plastic panels above and below the steering column.

Laine cursed her hands, which were shaking even harder now, and despite her out-of-control heartbeat and breathing, she tried to tamp down her responses. Hard to do with that with those bullets eating their way through the car. Even if she managed to hotwire it, those bullets might have already disabled the engine.

It took some doing, but she finally managed to get the panel off, and some wires spilled out.

"Take the red one—" Tucker's explanation was cut off by more shots.

Different from those that had been coming at them.

Laine hadn't thought the noise from the gunfight could get any worse, but she'd obviously been wrong.

She glanced out at Darren again to see if he was responsible for this new round of gunfire, but he was still in place against the antiques store. He was holding his gun in both hands against his chest with the barrel pointed up. The stance of a man who was waiting, not firing.

"Disconnect the red wire from the cylinder," Tucker continued. "And strip off the plastic ends." His voice was calm enough, but she saw the concern in his eyes. If she didn't get the cruiser started soon so they could escape, they'd be killed.

That gave her another shot of adrenaline that she desperately needed. Laine used the knife again to start scraping off the plastic. She'd barely gotten started when Tucker's phone rang.

"It's Reed," she told Tucker. She put the call on speaker and kept working on stripping the wires. Obviously she wouldn't make a good car thief because she was working at a snail's pace.

"There's a second shooter," Reed said the moment he came on the line. "And he's covering the rear roof. The guards can't get close enough to take out either of the men."

Tucker cursed. Laine groaned. She kept working.

"Tell the guards to stay in place and wait for a shot," Tucker told the deputy. In the same breath, he tipped his head to the wires again. "Twist the ends together, but don't let it touch anything else. Then strip the brown wire."

Even though the instructions were simple, the shots were more than enough of a distraction to make the task next to impossible. Laine grabbed the brown wire just as a shot slammed through the engine and made it all the way into the interior. It nicked the sleeve of her shirt.

Maybe her arm, too, since she felt the stinging pain.

That didn't stop her. In fact, it caused her to speed up, and the moment she had the brown wire stripped and the ends tied together, she glanced over at Tucker.

"What now?" she asked.

"I'll finish it." That was the only warning she got before he finally climbed into the cruiser and threw himself across the seat.

Laine hadn't ended the call, so she could still hear Reed yelling something. And she could also hear another voice.

Hague's.

That put her heart in her throat, and she hoped the man wasn't launching some kind of attack inside the sheriff's office. But she also heard something else.

A scream.

Not from Hague. This was from a woman, and Laine couldn't be sure, but it sounded like Rhonda. Mercy, had all their suspects managed to converge on this spot?

And if so, why?

It was a sickening thought that they could all be in this together. But if that were true, why would they have shown up right in the middle of this attack?

Ignoring the scream, Tucker touched the ends of the wires together. There was a spark, and the engine roared to life. Laine said a quick prayer of thanks that the bullets hadn't damaged it. He didn't waste even a moment maneuvering himself behind the wheel.

"Hold on," Tucker warned her.

There was no clear spot left on the windshield for him to see, but he hit the accelerator, and the cruiser practically flew out of the parking lot. There were no oncoming vehicles, thank goodness—probably because the sound of those gunshots had kept everyone at bay.

The bullets kept coming at them, even as the cruiser screeched away from the diner. The shooters adjusted their positions and continued to fire, but the bullets didn't go into the interior of the car.

They went into the tires.

Laine couldn't be sure, but it felt as if at least two tires had been shot out. Tucker had no choice but to bring the cruiser to a stop, and he got out.

"Stay on the floor," he warned her, and he started back toward the diner.

"It's too dangerous for you to do this," Laine called out to him.

"I won't go far. Can't risk those shooters coming out here to kidnap you."

That caused the skin on the back of her neck to crawl. The killer had come too close to taking her last time, and if they were bold enough to attempt another attack in broad daylight, then they'd have no problem gunning down Tucker and anyone else who got in their way.

Tucker kept a firm grip on his gun and shooting wrist as he inched away from the car. There were no more sounds of shots. Just eerie silence punctuated by an occasional shout.

Laine tried to keep watch. Tried to keep the panic in check, too. Still no shots. She figured it was too much to hope that the guards had managed to capture them. It was more likely that the shooters were on the move.

"You'd better be down," Tucker said to her over his shoulder, and he pivoted in the direction of one of the buildings just up the street from the diner.

He fired.

Tucker immediately jumped to the side behind a concrete park bench. Laine couldn't see who or what he was aiming at, but she certainly heard what followed.

Shots.

Not just a couple of them, but enough to make an all-out gunfight. And they were close. Maybe just yards away.

She put her hands over her ears to muffle the noise, but she kept watch of Tucker. "Stay put!" she yelled, though she doubted he even heard her.

He certainly didn't listen if he did, because he took aim again and fired off another shot.

This time she saw something. A man staggering out from the alley between two buildings. He was dressed all in black and was carrying some kind of rifle. Definitely not someone from the diner. No, this was almost certainly one of their attackers.

"He's headed right for you!" someone shouted, and it took her a second to realize it was Reed's voice coming from the phone.

"The gunman's coming your way," she warned Tucker.

Again, he took aim, but before Tucker could even pull the trigger, someone else fired.

The shot blasted through the air.

Chapter Thirteen

Tucker heard the shot, and for a split second, he thought he was a dead man.

No pain, no feeling of having a bullet blasting through him. It took him another split second to figure out what the heck was going on.

Ahead of him, he spotted Darren, his gun still drawn, and he had his attention nailed to the man on the ground to the right of him.

The second shooter.

And someone that Tucker might not have spotted in time before he got off a shot. But Darren had obviously seen and shot him.

"Don't get out of the car yet," Tucker said to Laine. "And call the ranch to make sure everything's okay there."

Tucker spared her a glance from over his shoulder to make sure she'd heard him. She had. But she was ghostly pale and shaking. Laine had come way too close to dying—again—and while Tucker needed to make sure she was all right, he first had to be certain that the threat had been neutralized.

And that the threat wasn't still standing directly in front of him.

Darren moved toward the man on the ground. Tucker

made his way to the gunman he'd shot, keeping his eye on Darren.

When Tucker reached the gunman, he knew he was dead.

Tucker didn't even have to check for a pulse to know that, or to notice that it was the same man who'd tried to kidnap Laine back at his place. After what the moron had done to her, it was hard to wish this had turned out differently, but a dead man couldn't tell them why he'd done it.

Or who'd hired him.

Even though on the surface, it appeared that Darren had helped him, had maybe even saved his life, Tucker wasn't about to dismiss him as a suspect just yet. Once the two jail guards had made it to the diner, it was highly likely that the gunmen would either be killed or taken captive.

Their boss definitely wouldn't have wanted the latter. Better dead than talking and naming names.

"How bad is Laine hurt?" Darren asked.

The question threw Tucker for a moment. Her ex's concern could have been real or faked—that wasn't what threw Tucker. It was the tone that Darren used, like that of a man who was certain she'd been injured. Or worse.

Tucker reeled around and looked past the lack of color in her face to the blood on the sleeve of her pale blue blouse.

"Call an ambulance," he shouted to Reed.

Hopefully, the deputy could hear Tucker's order. And hopefully, an ambulance was already on the way. Surely someone in that diner had called 911.

Despite the fact he had an armed suspect nearby, Tucker ran back to Laine and crawled into the shot-out cruiser with her.

"I'm fine," she insisted, probably because he looked ready to lose it. "So is everyone at the ranch. I just talked to Colt, and he said there's been no sign of attackers."

That was good, but it was the only good thing about this mess.

"You're not fine. You're bleeding." It turned his stomach to see that blood, and he ripped open her sleeve so he could see just how bad it was.

"It's a scratch. The bullet just grazed me."

"And you didn't say anything." Yeah, he definitely sounded like a man on the verge of losing it.

Tucker forced himself to take a deep breath. Forced himself to look at this like a lawman and not like some guy who'd, well, kissed her. The wound didn't appear to be serious. It was a graze, as she'd said. But she still needed to see a doctor.

"I'm sorry," Tucker managed to say.

"Sorry for saving my life?" Laine huffed, and in an instant her color got a whole lot better. "*Right*. Don't you dare apologize for what just happened. There's no way you could have stopped this."

Not true. If he could just get to the bottom of this investigation and arrest the idiot who'd put her life in danger yet again. It would happen. He would find this piece of dirt and make him, or her, pay hard.

Tucker heard the wail of the ambulance. Not just one from the sound of it, but several. Good. He had no idea if anyone else was hurt, but there was plenty of potential for civilian injuries with all those shots that'd been fired.

"Just wait until the ambulance gets here," Tucker told Laine when she started to get out. "I need to make sure this is finished."

And *finishing* it started with Darren.

"What the heck were you doing out here?" Tucker demanded, his narrowed gaze zooming right in on the man.

"I got a text saying there was trouble going down, and that you were going to use that trouble to set me up."

Tucker wasn't sure whether to curse or laugh. "Who sent that?"

Darren shook his head. "The name and number were blocked."

Now Tucker did curse. "And you believed anything an anonymous source had to say after your girlfriend was murdered and her body was dumped on your ranch?"

Tucker let his question hang in the air and thought about just how stupid—or calculating—Darren had been. For now, he motioned for Darren to hand over his gun.

"Really, we're gonna do this?" Darren challenged.

"Yeah," Tucker said with attitude, tapping the badge on his shirt.

One way or another, Darren was handing over that gun. No way did Tucker want an armed suspect wandering around to pick off him and Laine.

"I'll want it back when you're finished playing lawman." Scowling and cursing, Darren handed him the gun, and Tucker put it in the back waist of his jeans.

The two ambulances pulled to a stop, and the medics darted out. So did Laine, and despite Tucker warning her to stay put, she walked toward them.

"I'm okay," she insisted again. She held up his phone. "But Reed's not. There's a problem in the sheriff's office."

Of course there was. Nothing about this day was going to be easy.

"Don't go far," Tucker ordered Darren, and he gently looped his arm around Laine's waist so he could get her moving toward the ambulance.

"This can wait," Laine said, leading him toward the sheriff's office instead. "Reed needs you now."

"Is someone hurt or dead?" he snarled. The moment he asked the question, Tucker knew exactly what'd happened. "Buford escaped."

She nodded. "And Hague ran out, too, supposedly to chase after him."

Great. Just what he didn't need. A suspect trying to help round up a fugitive.

Tucker hoped Laine was right about being able to wait to get to the hospital, because he didn't take her directly to the ambulance. However, he did motion for one of the medics to follow them into the sheriff's office.

Yeah, it was chaos inside, all right. Reed was on the phone, yelling for someone to send out a search crew. Rhonda was sitting in the chair next to his desk, sobbing. Twin steaks of mascara tears streaked down her cheeks. The gun cabinet was open, and papers were scattered on the floor.

Another dark-haired man dressed in a suit paced the floor. Hague's lawyer, no doubt. His cold, gray eyes landed on them as if he blamed them for the shooting and his client's hasty departure. Tucker glared back. He wasn't in the mood to take anyone else's mess off their hands. Especially someone who had Hague for a client.

"What happened?" Tucker asked Reed the moment he finished his call. He holstered his gun, eased Laine into one of the other chairs and again motioned to the medic to tend to her. The guy hurried right over.

"I was at the window, trying to get a clean shot at the gunman on the roof when she came running in." Reed tipped his head to Rhonda. "Then she started screaming."

"That prisoner came out of the room," Rhonda said

through a sob, "and he worked his hands around his lawyer's neck so that his chains and cuffs were choking her. He dragged her out the back door like she was a rag doll."

Hell. He should have seen this coming. In fact, this entire attack could have been designed just to free Buford. Now Buford had a hostage.

Maybe.

And maybe the lawyer had been in on this, too, and had just been pretending to be his captive so she could get him out of there.

"Did Buford manage to get a gun?" Tucker asked.

Reed shook his head. "But Hague grabbed one. He said he wasn't going to let that innocent woman get hurt."

That was admirable, if it was the truth. With all the other insanity going on, it was possible that Hague took the gun so he could give it to Buford.

"I tried to talk my client out of this," the pacing suit said.

"And you are?" Tucker snapped.

"Steve Wilkey," he spat out, as if it wasn't any of Tucker's business.

"Well, Mr. Wilkey, your client has earned you a little stay here until we can get all of this sorted out."

As expected, that didn't put a pleasant expression on the man's sour face. His expression got significantly worse when Tucker led him down the hall and locked him in one of the interview rooms. He couldn't hold him for long, and the guy was already making a call before Tucker stepped away. Still, it would get Hague's eyes and ears away from Rhonda in case the woman had anything else to tell them.

"Right after the attack started, I called the sheriff from Appaloosa Pass," Reed continued. "He's sending over all his available deputies. The Rangers are sending someone, too. They should be here soon."

Good. That was a start, and Tucker hoped that *soon* would be soon enough. "Buford shouldn't be hard to find. He's wearing an orange jumpsuit and is cuffed at the hands and feet. He can't get far like that."

Well, unless someone had a vehicle waiting nearby to whisk him away. Which was entirely possible.

Tucker took out his phone and called the Ranger crime lab to make sure they were on their way. They were. And with that taken care of, he turned his attention back to Laine.

She was making a face, and it took him a moment to realize it was because the medic was dabbing her arm with antiseptic. She softened her expression when she caught him looking at her.

"I'm fine," she repeated.

"She is," the medic agreed. He took out a bandage strip and pressed it to the wound on her arm. "It's just a deep scratch, but as a precaution, she should drop by her doctor's office and get a tetanus shot."

"I will," Laine mumbled. She pointed to the diner. "Now, go take care of the people who really might be hurt."

The medic waited for Tucker to give him the nod before he rushed out. Hopefully, there wouldn't be any injuries, but at the very least, some folks would be in shock.

Maybe Laine was, too.

She suddenly looked very calm for a woman who'd come close to dying. It wouldn't last. Tucker figured she was holding herself together for his sake, so he wouldn't feel like kicking himself for allowing something like this to happen again.

"You want me to go out there and check on things?" Reed asked, volleying glances between Rhonda and Laine.

Tucker nodded. "Just make sure the back door and windows are locked." Buford likely wouldn't come back, but Tucker didn't want to risk him, or anyone else for that matter, having another go at trying to kill Laine. "And get Darren's phone. I need to check something on it."

Once Reed was outside, Laine stood and pushed her hair from her face. "I'll get you out of here as soon as possible," he promised.

"And I'll leave, too," Rhonda insisted. "As soon as it's safe."

Heaven knew when that would be.

"Why'd you come back to the sheriff's office?" Tucker asked her.

"My car wouldn't start." Rhonda's breath broke and she wiped away more tears. "I'd parked up the street in the grocery store lot, and I got worried that maybe someone had tampered with the engine. I came back so I could ask you to check it for me."

Either it was another bad coincidence, or Rhonda had come back to watch her hired guns in action. Of course, that would pretty much make her a psycho.

Something he couldn't completely rule out.

"I didn't know my cousin would be here," Rhonda went on, "or I wouldn't have come. I don't like the things Martin's been saying about me."

Tucker figured Hague felt the same way about her. But which one of them had reason for concern?

Maybe neither.

Tucker glanced out the window at their third suspect, Darren, who was handing over his phone to Reed. Darren clearly wasn't happy about that, and as soon as he slapped it in Reed's hand, he started to pace on the sidewalk.

"By any chance, did you call Darren earlier?" he asked Rhonda.

"No." Her forehead bunched up. "Why, did he say I did?"

"No. Just wondering."

She stared at him, the tears welling up in her eyes again. "Darren did say that I had. I don't know why people always accuse me of things I didn't do."

Her hands were shaking like crazy, but she clutched her purse against her chest like a shield. Tucker nearly drew his gun again when she reached inside. But instead of a weapon, she pulled out a bottle of firecracker-red polish and proceeded to give her nails another coat.

Rhonda followed Laine's gaze to her hands. "I saw you looking at my nails when I was in here earlier. Couldn't figure out why at first, but it was because of the manicure, wasn't it?" She didn't wait for an answer. "It's just something I do when I'm stressed. It's like you looking at Sergeant McKinnon."

Tucker blinked. "Excuse me?"

"Laine always looks at you when she's stressed. Like the conversation we had with Darren—whenever something hit a nerve with her, she'd look at you. You're like her security blanket or something."

He glanced at Laine to see if this made a lick of sense. Tucker didn't get much of an answer. Just a deer-caught-in-headlights look from Laine, and even that vanished when two people approached the door.

Reed and Darren.

Since Tucker didn't trust Darren any farther than he could throw him, he stepped in front of Laine and put his hand on the butt of his gun. He'd already taken Darren's gun, but that didn't mean the man didn't have a backup.

Coming through the door, Darren scowled at Tucker's stance. Tucker just scowled back. No way was he going to apologize for protecting Laine.

Reed handed Tucker the man's phone and then stepped away to make a call. Tucker scrolled through the recent calls on Darren's phone until he got to one with an unknown name and number. It'd been made about an hour earlier—just about when those gunmen would have been setting up their attack.

"I told you the person blocked the name and number. Satisfied?" Darren took back his phone. "I think after everything that just happened, I should take the babies to my ranch where I can keep them safe. When you get the DNA results back—"

"I got the results," Tucker interrupted. He tried to figure out a good way to share them, and just decided to blurt it out. "Dawn's the mother, but you're not the father."

Darren looked as if someone had slugged him. "You're lying."

Tucker shook his head. "DNA proves otherwise. Their father's a convicted murderer named Kurt Laverty. Did Dawn ever mention him?"

"No." Darren scrubbed his hand over his face and dropped down in one of the chairs. "I guess Dawn lied to me."

"Yeah. I'm sorry about that." And he was. Tucker knew how he would feel if he'd thought those kids were his, only to learn they were someone else's, and they were about to be legally snatched away.

"Some good news," Reed announced. "The medic said no one else was hurt in the shooting."

Tucker blew out a breath of relief, a breath that would have been a whole lot bigger if Buford had been caught. The man was a killer and would no doubt try to kill again if he wasn't stopped.

"Go ahead and start taking statements," Tucker said to Reed, and he helped Laine to her feet. "I need to check on some…things."

Laine herself was one of those things, but he also needed to call Egan Caldwell, a Ranger friend. The minute he had her in the break room, Tucker checked her arm. Because of the pristine white bandage now covering it, he could no longer see that angry-looking cut, but the images of it in his head were way too clear.

"Don't say you're sorry again," she blurted out, and Laine came up on her tiptoes and brushed a kiss over his lips.

Tucker hadn't known just how much he needed that kiss until she gave it to him. He eased his arm around her and kissed her right back.

Yeah. It was what he had needed all right, and judging from the little sound Laine made, she had needed it, too. And that wasn't good. They had enough going on without adding kisses. That's why he stopped this time, but Tucker wasn't the sort of man who lied to himself.

He would kiss her again.

And more. They'd soon land in bed to take up where they'd left off all those years before. Later, that is. For now, he had to tell her something, and he was really going to have to sell it.

"I need to arrange a safe house for the babies," he started. "One away from us. It doesn't have to be far, but they can't be under the same roof as us."

Tucker got the reaction he figured he'd get. Her shoulders slumped, and her mouth began to tremble. "We've kept them safe so far."

"Yeah. But we've gotten lucky. We can't continue to rely on luck when it comes to them. With Buford out there again, he or his boss could already be planning another attack on us. He wants us dead, and I don't want the twins getting caught in the middle of another gunfight."

Hell, he didn't want Laine caught in one, either. That cut on her arm was proof of just how close these morons had come to killing her. Next time, it could be a thousand times worse.

"I'm the one the killers want most," she said. "You need to distance yourself from me."

Oh, man.

The tears came again, and Tucker pulled her back into his arms.

"I'm not doing that, okay? They want us both. Those shots today proved that." He shook his head. "For now, we stay together and try to figure out who's behind this. Once we've done that, there'll be no need for the babies to be in a safe house."

She seemed relieved, for a moment anyway, but then she had to blink back tears. "How soon would the twins be moved?"

Best not to sugarcoat it. "Pretty much now."

He stepped a few feet away from her and called Egan. It wasn't exactly a surprise call. Tucker had contacted him the night before and asked him to make preliminary arrangements. It was time to make those arrangements final.

"I just heard about the shooting," Egan said the moment he answered the call.

"Yeah. We need to move the babies ASAP. Don't tell me where you're taking them."

Tucker didn't think there were any leaks in the sheriff's office, but he didn't want to take any chances. Buford had had access to that particular room since he'd used the back door to escape, and Tucker didn't want to risk Buford or his lawyer planting some kind of eavesdropping device.

"Just promise me the babies will be safe," Tucker added to Egan.

"They will be. I'll get a team out to your family's ranch now to pick them up, and we'll drive them to the safe house."

So everything was set into motion. Well, partly, anyway. "I want to see them before the Ranger moves them," Laine insisted.

Tucker didn't argue with her. He wanted her out of there anyway, but he had to make sure everything was as secure as he could make it.

When he went back into the squad room, he saw that Reed was on the phone. Rhonda and Darren were seated and writing their statements. Better yet, a guard from the jail and the night deputy had come in to help.

Good.

That freed him up to get Laine back to the ranch.

"Call if you need me," Tucker said to Reed. "And once we're out of here, then you can let Hague's lawyer go." He started for the door.

Reed held up his hand in a "wait a second" gesture. Tucker couldn't tell who the deputy was talking to, but judging from his expression, this wasn't good news.

"How bad?" he asked, the moment Reed finished his call.

"Bad." Reed drew in a long, weary breath. "We've got two dead bodies on our hands."

Chapter Fourteen

Laine's heart dropped when Tucker pulled in front of the Sweetwater Ranch. There was no sign of the Ranger team who'd come and collected the twins, and that meant she hadn't been able to see them.

Maybe for the last time.

It shouldn't have felt like a big deal since they weren't hers. Might never be. And it wasn't as if she didn't have other things to occupy her mind, especially after the news of the two dead bodies. A horrible ending to what had been a horrible attack.

One had been Penny Wilmer, Buford's attorney.

Her body had been found on the side of the road just outside of town. Since they'd known that Buford had taken her hostage, it wasn't a total shock. Still, it'd been a reminder that they were dealing with killers.

And one of those killers had been killed.

Tucker and she didn't have all the details yet, but it appeared that someone had gotten past the guard at the hospital who was watching the injured gunman, Hines, and had given the man a lethal injection. He could no longer tell them the identity of the person who'd hired him or any details about the black-market baby operation.

Neither could the man who'd launched the attack from

the roof of the diner because he was dead, too. Reed had shown Laine a photo of the dead man, just to verify it was their missing gunman who'd tried to kidnap her at Tucker's place. It was.

Now, Buford was the only one who could give them those details, and they'd have to find him first. So far, there'd been no sign of him.

"I'm sorry," Tucker said as he brought the truck to a stop in front of the house.

He didn't have to clarify that apology. Laine knew. He, too, seemed sorry that they'd missed saying good-bye to the babies.

"You're sure they'll be safe with the Rangers?" Laine asked him.

"Yeah. And the babies will be well cared for. The team has a nanny from the Safe Cradle Agency."

An agency that Laine knew well. It provided body-guard nannies to at-risk infants and children. Sadly, the twins definitely fell into that category.

Because she and Tucker were also in danger, he didn't waste any time getting her into the house. Colt was in the foyer, waiting for them.

"The Rangers left about ten minutes ago," Colt said, checking his watch. "Now that you're back, I need to head to the office and help Reed. There's a mountain of paperwork from the two murders."

Tucker nodded. "Thanks for everything." He glanced around the empty rooms that flanked the foyer. "Where are the others?"

"Rosalie went up to her room. Mary, too. They were a little upset to see the babies leave. Dad's out with one of the hands checking on some new calves."

Colt headed for the door, and the moment he was outside, Tucker locked up and set the security system. "Come on," Tucker added. "You've got to get some rest."

Laine was too exhausted to argue, and besides, the look on his face was troubled enough without her adding more to it by protesting.

"I know you don't want to worry about me," she mumbled as they worked their way up the stairs. "And you don't have to. I'm not going to fall apart or anything."

She hoped.

Tucker made a noncommittal sound that rumbled deep in his throat, and he just kept her moving until they reached the guest room. Laine expected him to deposit her inside and head to the ranch office to work, but he stepped inside with her.

"Rest," he ordered, tipping his head to the bed.

She blindly started in that direction, but then stopped and placed her hand on the side of his face. "Rest would do you some good, too."

His eyebrow moved up, and she knew what his answer would be. No way. Tucker would work himself into the ground to try to make things right.

But maybe she could do something about that.

Without thinking it through, Laine came up on her toes and brushed her mouth over his. She should have thought it through. Or rested, as Tucker had ordered. Because she'd only meant for it to be a kiss of comfort.

However, their kisses weren't the comforting sort.

Nope. Just the simple touch sent a lightning bolt of heat through her entire body. It probably didn't have that same kind of impact on Tucker, but it did put some fire in his eyes.

"Really?" he challenged.

She lifted her shoulder. "I figure I've made so many

mistakes already. Going to the baby farm with the CI. Getting involved with Darren. Running to you for help. What's one more?"

He didn't lift his eyebrow this time, but he did tighten his mouth. "You think coming to me was a mistake?"

"Of course." Not that she'd had other solid options, but she should have come up with something. *Anything.* "Buford wouldn't have tried to kill you if I'd managed to go to someone else."

"No, he would just have tried to kill that *someone else.*" Tucker mumbled some profanity, slipped his arm around her waist and eased her to him. "So, no mistake there. But the other three things, yeah, definite mistakes."

She flinched a little. "You lumped that kiss in with those other huge mistakes?"

He stared down at her. "Yeah, because it wasn't just a kiss. You're tired. I'm tired. Our defenses are way down, and anything including a simple kiss will feel as if it's full-blown foreplay."

Laine couldn't argue with that, either. Her nerves were right there at the surface, and it would feel so good to lose herself in Tucker's arms.

In his bed.

The timing was all wrong, though.

She shook her head, rethinking that. The timing would always be wrong with Tucker. His mother's trial would start soon, bringing all those old memories to the surface. While neither she nor Tucker seemed to have much emotional stake in the outcome of all that, it would mean having to deal with their families' reactions.

Especially her mother's.

And his father's. And those of half of his siblings.

"Talking yourself out of it, huh?" Tucker drawled.

She started to nod, but rethought that, too. The timing would never be good for them. Her family was never going to accept him, and the same was true for his accepting her. Besides, there was no telling when this investigation might be over.

No telling when they'd have a chance to be alone again like this.

Or when she'd have an opportunity to add another mistake to the ones she'd already made.

Laine reached up, slid her hand around the back of Tucker's neck and pulled him down to her. No hesitation. No resistance. From either of them.

Just the sizzling kiss that she knew meant there was no more turning back.

TUCKER HAD SOME serious doubts about this. Man, did he. But he just shoved those doubts aside and kept on kissing Laine as if he had a right to do just that.

He didn't.

The only thing he had a right to do was protect her, and while kissing her wouldn't do that, Tucker couldn't see any way around it.

Laine and he had been eyeing each other for a while now, and the heat had been building with each passing second. He'd have an easier time stopping his lungs from needing air than he would putting a stop to this.

So, knowing he was making a huge mistake, Tucker decided to make it worth whatever the hell price they were going to pay for this. And there would be a price. Laine was all worked up now, but soon she'd realize it was impossible for the two of them to be together.

That put a knot in his gut, and gave him a few much-needed seconds of hesitation. He pulled back just a little, his gaze meeting hers.

"What?" she said, her voice warm and breathy. "Please tell me you're not stopping."

"No."

But Tucker likely would have given a little more thought to that *no chance of making this work* notion if she hadn't latched onto his neck and pulled him back to her for a kiss. She didn't stop there. Laine pushed up his shirt, her hand landing on his chest.

Heck, that did it.

No more time for thoughts or doubts. He deepened the kiss and did some shirt-tugging of his own.

Tucker pulled off her top and sent it sailing over his shoulder. He got a good look at those curves that'd been driving him crazy. A good taste, too, when he lowered his head to kiss the tops of her breasts.

Oh, man. He'd figured this would be good, but he'd way underestimated it. She was perfect—not just her breasts, but the rest of her, too.

Laine made a helpless little sound of surrender, and she sagged against him. Tucker pinned her against the closed door and kept kissing her until soon, very soon, it wasn't enough.

The lacy white bra went next, and he got a punch of sizzling heat when he kissed her bare breasts. And lower, to her stomach.

Laine made more of those sounds when his mouth reached the front of her jeans. He unzipped them, pulling them off her. Her panties, too. The next kiss caused her moans to get significantly louder.

"Get up here," she mumbled, grabbing onto his shoulders and hauling him back up the length of her body. "I want us to do this together, with you inside me."

Tucker had no objections to that, but he was more than a little concerned that *together* was going to happen pretty darn fast. Laine didn't just tug at his clothes. She started fighting to get him undressed, and Tucker intended to help her do just that.

But she stopped him with a kiss.

Her clever mouth landed on his neck, just below his right ear, and Tucker darn near lost what little breath he had left. He was rock-hard and ready, but that did it.

For just a moment, he allowed himself to get lost in the heat. In those neck kisses she was so good at giving. He hadn't needed anything else to fire him up, but Laine delivered anyway.

While she continued to grapple with his jeans and make him crazier with those neck kisses, Tucker maneuvered her away from the door, somehow remembering to lock it. They moved together without stopping the kisses and without breaking the hold they had on each other. By the time they made it to the bed, Tucker was sure he was hot enough to burn to ash.

"Now," she insisted.

He couldn't have delayed this if he'd tried, but he did hope there would be a second round somewhere in their future. One not driven by this insanity to finish all of this at lightning speed.

Laine finally got him unzipped just as they dropped down on the mattress. A new wrestling match began, and they managed to get off his boots so the jeans could go next. However, Tucker put another pause to the frantic pace when he caught sight of a naked Laine beneath him.

Yeah, she was a beauty, all right.

Over the years when he hadn't been able to stop it, he'd imagined her like this. Naked, beneath him, flushed with arousal and waiting for him to take her. Good thing they didn't have a lot of time, because he had to have her *now*.

Clearly, Laine felt the same way. She slid her legs around the back of his, and Tucker had no choice but to sink deep and hard into her.

His vision blurred.

His heart started galloping a mile a minute.

Everything inside him urged him to finish this and bring them both to a climax, but even through the crazy haze of fire in his head, he knew this wasn't just sex.

Hell.

Tucker wanted to remind her that he wasn't the more-than-sex type. But he didn't get the chance to say anything. He started to move inside her, and every logical thought flew right out of his head.

The only thing that mattered now was taking Laine.

"You're much too good at this," she mumbled, matching him thrust for thrust.

Tucker wanted to say something, anything, but he was past the point of coherent speech. Past the point of anything except racing toward the finishing line. First for Laine. And then for himself.

The feel of her release roared through him. Driving him harder. Pushing him closer. Until he couldn't hang on to the pleasure even a second longer. The last thing Tucker heard before he went over was Laine.

Whispering his name.

Chapter Fifteen

The slow-burning hunger was finally quiet. For a little while, anyway. Laine's body was slack from the pleasure, but she had no doubts—*none*—that the sizzling need would return with a vengeance. Maybe in a day or two, when she and Tucker had this investigation under control.

Or sooner.

The heat trickled through her again when he lifted his head and looked down at her. She'd never been immune to that handsome face. Never would be. Those alarmingly good looks made her want him all over again.

Too bad it wasn't only his looks that drew her in.

Sadly, it was the man himself, the total package, and she wondered if she'd ever get over this thing she had for Tucker.

Probably not.

Making love with him had only strengthened her desire. And that meant she was setting herself up for a broken heart.

"Man," Tucker mumbled. "When I mess things up, I go for broke."

Laine dredged up a smile, located his mouth and kissed him. "I should probably be insulted by that."

He made a sound of disagreement. "You should probably slug me and toss me out of your bed."

Slugging and tossing Tucker were the last things she wanted. Well, unless he continued to talk like that. Yes, it was a mistake, but it certainly hadn't felt like one, and she wanted him to feel the same conflicted emotions she was—but not for another few minutes.

Tucker groaned, moved off her and flopped onto his back beside her. Laine braced herself for more chatter about how wrong all of that had been, but he merely leaned over and returned the kiss she'd given him earlier.

"I can't stay," he mumbled, easing off the bed.

And she wondered just how many times he had said that to a woman. Tucker certainly wasn't the sort to linger after landing in bed, but she'd hoped for a little more time.

Well, at least she had a view to admire.

Mercy. How could any man look that good with so little sleep, especially after all the stress they'd been through?

"I want to call Egan and make sure the twins arrived at the safe house," he added.

That got her moving off the bed, too. Laine certainly hadn't forgotten about the babies, but she hadn't thought they'd be able to contact them so soon. Or at all.

"Will they be there already?" she asked.

"Maybe. I doubt he'll take them too far away since there are several safe houses in the area. But if they haven't gotten to one of them yet, I'll find out when they're due to arrive and how much backup Egan has with him."

Good. She wanted every precaution to be taken. "A call will be secure?" The last thing she wanted was for the kidnappers to find the twins and go after them again.

"Our phones are secure." And he pressed the Ranger's number. Sergeant Egan Caldwell answered on the first ring.

"We're still driving around," he volunteered. "The kiddos are fine."

Laine prayed that it would stay that way.

"Someone did try to follow us," the Ranger went on. "The guy was darn persistent, too, but I managed to lose him about fifteen minutes ago."

Had her heart stopped for a few seconds? It'd certainly felt like it. She'd known the kidnappers were likely watching them. Would perhaps try to follow them, too. But it was gut-wrenching to hear it spelled out.

"You're certain you lost the guys following you?" Tucker asked Egan.

"Positive. And I won't go anywhere near the safe house until I'm sure they haven't picked up our trail. It's not that far from town so I'll call you once I have everyone settled."

Tucker thanked him and ended the call, but then he just stared at the phone. The muscles in his jaw started to work hard against each other.

"If you decide to adopt them, I'll help." He didn't exactly look comfortable with that offer, but when his eyes met hers, Laine could see that it was genuine. "Not that I know much about babies, but—"

"But you care for them," she finished for him. "I understand."

Her mind immediately started to weave a fantasy. Of the two of them taking care of the babies together. Of them landing in bed for another mind-blowing round of lovemaking. But Laine forced aside those images. Tucker's offer certainly hadn't included playing house with her.

Had it?

The fantasy took off again like a bee-stung horse, but this time it was the sound of Tucker's phone that nipped it in the bud. Laine's attention snapped to the screen, where she thought she might see Sergeant Caldwell's name, but instead she saw Colt's.

"We found Buford," Colt announced the moment Tucker answered.

Both fear and relief jolted through her. She wanted the monster found, but Laine prayed he was nowhere near the babies.

"Where is he?" Tucker asked his brother.

"At your house."

Laine did a mental double take. Tucker's house was only a quarter mile away. Way too close.

The muscles in Tucker's face tightened again. "Please tell me you have him under arrest."

"Not yet. One of the deputies from Appaloosa Pass spotted Buford and went in pursuit. Buford ditched his truck not far from the ranch and ran on foot through the pasture to get to your house. He's inside, but we have him surrounded. Some of the ranch hands are coming to help so Buford won't be able to sneak out."

"Good. I'll be there in a few minutes." Tucker ended the call and immediately finished dressing. "You'll stay here," he insisted before she could say a word.

Not that Laine wanted to go with him. But she also didn't want him rushing out into possible gunfire.

Even if it was his job.

She got a solid reminder of that when he put on his shirt, badge attached, and then slid on his shoulder holster. As if it were the most natural thing in the world, he dropped another kiss on her mouth, and Laine had to hurry to keep up with him when he rushed out of the room and down the stairs.

"Reset the security system and stay away from the windows when you go back up to your room," Tucker instructed at the front door. "I'll call my dad and let him know what's going on so he can come upstairs and stay with you. Rosalie's in the house, too."

He rattled off the security code, and just like that, Tucker was gone.

Laine watched him from one of the sidelight windows. It was already dusk, but she had no trouble seeing him get into one of the trucks parked alongside the house. And he wasn't alone. Two armed ranch hands got in with him, and they sped away. Another ranch hand stayed, standing guard in front of the house.

She hadn't realized she was shaking until she locked the door and pressed in the security code. Once she had that done, Laine didn't waste any time getting upstairs. She turned off the lights, and despite the fact she wanted to see if she could spot Tucker's place from any of the windows, she stayed back.

And she waited.

The seconds crawled by. So did the thoughts in her suddenly wild imagination.

This time it was not a fantasy of playing house with Tucker, but rather a stream of images of another gunfight. She seriously doubted that Buford would just surrender, and that meant Tucker, his brother and anyone else out there were in danger because Buford would have come armed and ready to kill.

Since she couldn't see what was going on, Laine tried to level her breathing so she could hear. Tucker's place was just up the road. Thankfully, she didn't hear any gunshots.

Laine was so focused on listening for those shots that she nearly jumped out of her skin when there was a knock at the door. She eased it open to see Tucker's father. He had a gun tucked in the waist of his jeans.

Roy slipped a phone into her hand. "Tucker said he'd call you on this number when he had Buford."

"Thanks." She must have looked even more terrified than she felt because Roy gave her arm a gentle pat. A generous gesture, considering what had gone on between their families.

"I'll be in my room right across the hall." He started to turn, but then he stopped and caught her gaze. "I'm old but I'm not blind. I can see what's happening between Tucker and you."

Uh-oh. She braced herself for another lecture like the one her mother had given her, but that wasn't a lecturing look in Roy's eyes.

"For what it's worth, I've always thought you were a good woman. Good for Tucker, too."

Laine had to stop her mouth from dropping open.

"Neither of you can probably see that because of the way circumstances put you in the middle of a mountain-sized mess," Roy went on. "Still, if I were you, I wouldn't give up on him just yet."

She shook her head. "But what about the rest of your family?"

He lifted his shoulder, gave a weary sigh. "Sometimes folks don't know what's best for them until it knocks them upside the head."

They shared a smile so brief that when Roy walked away, Laine wasn't even sure it'd happened. Once Roy was inside his room, Laine went back into hers. However, she'd barely managed to get the door shut when she heard a sound.

Not gunfire.

This was a loud humming noise, and it took her a moment to realize what it was. The security alarm. Someone had opened a window or a door.

She forced herself not to panic. After all, Rayanne, Rosalie and Mary were in the house, and any one of them could have gone outside. She stepped into the hall, waiting for someone to punch in the access code so the humming wouldn't go to a full wail.

But that didn't happen.

The alarm blasted through the house, and Roy hurried out into the hall. Soon other doors opened, too, and Rosalie came out from the guest room that she'd been using when the babies had been at the ranch.

"Where's your sister?" Roy immediately asked.

Rosalie shook her head. "She went back over to the guesthouse right after the Rangers took the twins. She said something about going through some of Seth's notes for the trial. Mary's in town. As far as I know, we're the only ones here."

Roy hurried to the keypad on the wall near the front of the stairs. "Someone triggered the alarm in one of the downstairs windows."

That sent Laine's stomach to her knees. Rayanne and Mary wouldn't have come in that way. She grabbed her phone and saw that she had no service.

Had someone managed to jam it?

Laine knew there were devices that people could use to disrupt phone signals. There'd been news reports about them. Had that happened now? And if so, who'd done it?

"Mary? Rayanne?" Roy shouted. "Who's down there?"

No one answered.

But even over the screech of the alarm, Laine heard the footsteps on the stairs. Someone was coming directly toward them.

TUCKER STEPPED FROM his truck, and with the two ranch hands following, he made his way to Colt, who'd taken cover behind his sheriff's cruiser.

Parked next to Colt and also behind cover was the deputy from Appaloosa Pass. With two hands guarding the back of the house, hopefully there was no way Buford could escape.

"Any sign of where he is in the house?" Tucker asked his brother.

Colt shook his head. "But Deputy Grange said he saw him go in through the back door."

A door that Tucker had likely left unlocked in his hurry to get Laine and the babies out of there the last time Buford had paid them a visit. Not that a simple lock would have stopped a man like Buford, but it might have slowed him down enough for the deputy to make an arrest.

Or kill him.

"Deputy Grange said Buford seemed to be staggering when he ran inside," Colt added.

Tucker shook his head. "You mean staggering like a wounded man?"

"Maybe. He couldn't tell. But it's possible Buford hurt his ankle or something."

Too bad the injury hadn't been enough to make him collapse in the yard. Being inside put the man in the catbird seat since there were plenty of windows through which to take shots at them.

Colt glanced at Tucker and did a double take. "You okay?"

Tucker automatically scowled, since he really didn't want to be questioned about his state of mind. Or maybe it was the well-pleasured vibe he might be giving off. "Yeah. Well, okay for someone about to face down a killer. Why?"

"You just look funny, that's all." And Colt took another long glance.

Probably at Tucker's messed-up hair, wrinkled clothes and few missed buttons on his shirt. Tucker probably had Laine's scent all over him. A brother would pick up on that.

A smart brother would keep his mouth shut about it, though.

Especially since Laine was a topic on which Colt and he would probably never see eye to eye.

Heck, two days before Tucker and she hadn't seen eye to eye, either. Sex changed things. It broke down barriers. Put the past in a different perspective. It was also distracting the heck out of him at the worst possible time.

Obviously, Colt was a smart brother, because he didn't push the subject.

"Right before all of this happened, I got a call about the twins," Colt continued a moment later. He reached into the cruiser and took out a tear-gas-canister gun. "SAPD talked with Dawn's aunt. She's sixty-four and about to retire. She doesn't want to raise the twins."

Despite everything else going on, that was a relief. It would be for Laine, too, and he couldn't wait to tell her the news.

Except it might only be temporary good news.

"What about Laverty's family?" Tucker asked. After all, Laverty was the birth father, and his kin would have a say in custody. "Is it possible they'll want to claim the babies?"

"No next of kin. He has some distant cousins, all in jail. None of them would pass a background check, much less qualify to get custody of his offspring."

Again, that was good, and once he had Buford out of the house and back in custody, it might be something Laine and he could celebrate.

Maybe with more of that distracting sex.

"I can put the tear-gas canister through the front window or the side," his brother said. "Can't guarantee it won't cause something to catch on fire, though."

Yeah, Tucker already knew that, but he also didn't want this to turn into a long standoff. The sooner they got Buford out of there, the better, and the tear gas should send the killer running outside. With Buford's record, though, it was likely the man would come out shooting.

"Don't worry about the house. But if possible, I need him alive," Tucker reminded Colt. With the other gunmen and Buford's lawyer dead, this man was his best shot at learning the truth about who was behind these attacks.

Colt nodded, took aim and fired. The tear-gas canister crashed through the window to the right of the front door, and Tucker heard it clank to the floor. Seconds later, wispy white gas started to ooze through the gaping hole in the glass.

Tucker took aim, waited.

Only a few seconds passed, but he suddenly got a bad feeling about all of it.

Why wasn't Buford running out?

He glanced at the main house. Tucker could see the lights stabbing through the twilight, but the place was too far away to tell if anything was wrong. He reminded himself that his father and sisters were in there. If Buford had somehow managed to escape and get to that house, they'd protect Laine. And besides, if something went wrong, one of them would call him.

Still, the skin crawled on the back of his neck.

"I'm speeding this up," Tucker warned his brother. He fired a shot into the eaves of the house. Then another.

No response.

Certainly no sign of Buford.

Tucker waited another couple of seconds, hoping that the front door would burst open, and Buford would come staggering out.

He didn't.

"Something's not right," Tucker mumbled. He took out his phone and pressed Laine's number. No answer. He tried again with the house phone.

Nothing.

Hell. This was some kind of trap.

"Call me when you have Buford out of there," Tucker said to his brother, and he didn't wait for the ranch hands who'd come with him. He jumped back in his truck, started the engine and hit the gas.

In his rearview mirror, he saw Colt and the others moving toward the house, guns raised. Ready in case Buford came out shooting. Tucker hated to put this on other people's shoulders. Buford was his problem, and he wanted to be the one to take him down. But he couldn't ignore the fact that Laine and the rest of his family might be under attack.

The short drive seemed to take an eternity, and when

he pulled to a stop in front of the house, Tucker still didn't see signs that anything was wrong. However, the moment he threw open his truck door, his phone rang.

Colt's name popped up on the screen.

"You have Buford?" Tucker immediately asked.

"We have him, all right." Colt paused. "But he's dead."

Oh, man. That was not what he wanted to hear. "You had to shoot him?"

"No. I think he was poisoned or something. I haven't examined the body yet, but I can see him through the window. He's on the floor in the kitchen, and there's foam around his mouth. He looks like he had a seizure."

Both concern and relief roared through Tucker. On the one hand, this meant Buford couldn't come after Laine and the babies again. But it also meant someone had likely murdered the one man who could give Tucker answers.

Who'd done that?

"There's more," Colt went on. "You can thank Deputy Grange for spotting it. There are trip wires on both the front and back doors. Someone's rigged them with explosives. They're small enough to fit in a man's pocket, but they probably would have gone off if we'd barged in there. That's why I haven't had a good look at the body yet."

Hell. If this dirtbag had set explosives at his place, maybe he'd done the same at the main house.

Tucker looked up at his family's home again, and he heard something he damn sure didn't want to hear. First, the sound of the security alarm blaring, and over that, he heard something else.

Laine shouting.

"Get down!"

Her shout was followed by a gunshot.

Chapter Sixteen

Laine saw the shadowy figure at the top of the stairs. And the gun pointed directly at Roy.

She shouted for Roy to get down, and she tried to pull him into the room with her.

But it was already too late.

The person fired a shot at him.

Thankfully, the guy missed, but he took aim again at Roy.

Rosalie screamed, and both Laine and she shoved Roy into the guest room and shut the door. They locked it and moved to the side in case the gunman tried to shoot his way through.

Laine braced herself for more shots, but they didn't come. In fact, other than the security alarm, there were no sounds of any kind, including footsteps.

Was the killer trying to sneak up on them?

If so, he'd certainly lost the element of surprise. But maybe he was trying to figure out a way to get to them other than breaking down the door. After all, he had to figure that at least one of them would be armed.

Her pulse was racing now, and the air felt still, as if everything was holding its breath. Roy started to open the door, no doubt to have a look at what was going on in the hall, but Laine pulled him back.

She didn't hear footsteps, but something caught her attention. A smell.

"Smoke," she mumbled.

Oh, mercy. Had he set the place on fire? If so, that would explain why he hadn't come after them. It also meant they could be trapped.

"Laine?" someone called out. *Tucker.* The alarm quit clanging, probably because he'd put in the code to stop it. "Dad?"

There were still no shots, but Laine knew she had to do something in case Tucker was walking right into a setup. The person who'd set the fire could ambush him.

"There's someone in the house!" she shouted. She prayed that would help him get out of the path of any bullets this monster intended to send his way.

Was it Buford out there? Had he managed to escape from Tucker's house and come for them? If so, he wouldn't stop until Tucker or one of them forced him to.

"It's getting thicker," Rosalie said, tipping her head to the milky-gray smoke oozing beneath the door.

It was also getting harder for her to breathe, but Laine didn't know what to do about that. If they hurried out into the hall, they could all be shot. But they couldn't stay put, either, because they were starting to cough. Besides, the fire could consume the house and burn them alive.

"Don't shoot. I'm coming up," Tucker yelled. He, too, was coughing.

Laine pulled in her breath, waiting and praying. Without the blare from the alarm, she had no trouble hearing the racing footsteps on the stairs and in the hall.

"It's me," Tucker said through his coughs.

Laine threw open the door and was so relieved to see him that she had to fight from launching herself into his arms. Tucker didn't give her a chance to do that anyway, because he moved them away from the door again.

"Is anyone hurt?" he asked, giving all three of them a quick glance.

Laine shook her head. "The man fired a shot at your father."

Tucker cursed, gave his dad another look. "I didn't see anyone downstairs. Just the smoke."

"Where's the fire?" Roy immediately asked.

"Don't think there is one. Looks like this bozo set off some smoke bombs downstairs."

Part of her was relieved, but the smoke could turn out to be just as deadly as the fire if it meant they couldn't breathe.

"I think the phones are jammed," Laine told him as Tucker motioned for them to come out of the room. He kept his gun aimed in the direction of the stairs.

"Yeah, someone used a signal zapper, and it's not Buford's doing. He's dead back at my house."

The sickening dread raced through her. Laine certainly hadn't wanted to come face-to-face with Buford again, but if he wasn't the one doing this, then who was?

She had a horrible thought that they would soon find out.

Leading the way, Tucker hurried them up the hall and toward the stairs, where the smoke was the thickest. Roy started coughing so hard that Laine and Rosalie each took him by the arm and tried to keep up with Tucker. By the time they made it to the bottom, her lungs felt ready to burst, and her eyes were watering so badly that she couldn't see more than a few feet in front of her.

"Not that way," Tucker said when she reached for the front door.

Probably because he thought the killer was out there waiting for them. And he or she could be. The smoke could have been a ruse to draw them all out of the house and into the line of fire. But the ruse would also work if they all passed out from smoke inhalation.

Then they'd be sitting ducks for a killer.

Instead, Tucker hurried them toward the back of the house. Not to the kitchen, either, where she knew there was a door to the backyard.

With his attention firing all around them, they went into the family room, and he hurried to the window on the far exterior wall. The smoke was still thick—there was more than enough to keep them all coughing—but Tucker still didn't throw open the window to let in the fresh air.

"Keep watch behind us," he said to his father. Roy turned, pointed his gun in that direction.

Tucker looked out the window, eased it open and then shoved out the screen. The night breeze immediately started to pour in, and Laine gulped in several long breaths before Tucker climbed out. As he'd done in the hall, he looked around, his gun ready, and then motioned for them to come out.

Laine helped Rosalie through first. When it was her turn, she tried to hurry in case their attacker came after Roy. The moment they all had their feet on the ground, Tucker got them moving again.

They only made it a few steps before Tucker stopped, pivoted and took aim.

A shot cracked through the air.

TUCKER FIRED AT their attacker, who'd just leaned out from the corner of the house.

He missed.

But thankfully so did the shooter.

His bullet slammed into the ground, but Tucker figured the idiot would soon pull the trigger again.

And he did.

Another shot immediately came their way, and instead of shooting back this time, Tucker knew he had to get Laine and the others out of the line of fire.

"This way," Tucker shouted, and he caught onto Laine's arm to run toward a pair of oaks about ten yards away. They had only made it a few steps when the shots returned.

Man, did they.

They came at them nonstop.

The shooter was obviously using some kind of assault weapon to be able to get off that many rounds that fast. It also meant he wouldn't have to pause to reload anytime soon. That wasn't good news.

Tucker kept moving, and the moment he reached the trees, he dragged Laine to the ground so he could cover her and help his dad and Rosalie.

But his heart dropped.

Rosalie and his dad weren't there.

It took Tucker a moment to pick through the darkness to spot them. Alive, thank God. They'd gone in the other direction. Probably because of the path of those bullets around them. And they were now behind some shrubs and a large stone birdbath. It wasn't much cover, but at least they weren't out in the open.

Tucker wanted to call out to them, to ask if they

were okay, but if the shooter didn't have them pin-pointed, that would give away their position. Besides, his father was a smart man, and he knew how to defend himself. Still, Tucker didn't want him or Rosalie to have to do that.

Because Laine was pressed right against him, he could feel the tightened muscles in her body and could hear her ragged breaths.

"Shhh," he said, trying to soothe her. It didn't work.

She was obviously terrified, and so was he. He wished he could assure her that he'd get all of them out of this alive. But a reassurance now would be a lie.

Tucker took out his phone to call Colt, but then cursed when he saw that he had no service. Laine had been right about someone jamming the phones. It wasn't hard to do, but it meant their attacker had not only brought jamming equipment and an assault weapon, but had also likely been the one to set the explosives at Tucker's house.

This had not been a spur-of-the-moment attack. It'd been well planned, and that meant Tucker had no idea what other things this idiot could throw their way. Or how many goons he'd brought with him to finish the job.

The shots kept coming, all of them aimed at Laine and him. Each bullet tore through the trees. It wouldn't be long before the gunman chipped away at enough of their cover to do some serious damage.

But the angle of the shots was a little off.

Not by much. Just enough for Tucker to think this guy didn't want them dead. Well, not both of them, anyway. Still, even if he wasn't trying to kill them, it didn't mean a stray bullet wouldn't finish them off.

"I'm sorry," he mumbled to Laine.

She lifted her head just a fraction and glared up at him. "This wasn't your fault."

He disagreed. "I sure as heck didn't stop it from happening."

But he could do something about stopping it now. If he could just maneuver himself into a better position, he might be able to get off a decent shot and put an end to the triggerman.

Tucker knew the side yard like the back of his hand. There were more trees and shrubs, but nothing that would get him into a position to fire. His brother's house was about forty yards away and was still under construction. It would give Tucker the right angle, but the odds were sky-high that the shooter would see him and stop him before he made it there.

That left one of the vehicles.

Several trucks were parked on the grounds. None would be ideal, but he somehow had to make it work. The biggest problem with the plan was that it involved leaving Laine alone.

He hated that.

Because this moron could have someone else out there, waiting for him to make a move just like that. Still, Tucker would likely be able to shoot anyone who attempted to kidnap Laine again.

"Wait here and stay down," Tucker told Laine.

She immediately started shaking her head. "You're not going out there."

"I don't have much of a choice." He motioned toward his dad's truck, which was about halfway between where they were and the front of the house.

The head-shaking continued, and when it finally stopped, he saw the tears shimmering in her eyes.

Oh, man. Not tears. It tore at his heart to see her cry, but it would tear at him even more if he didn't do everything possible to get her out of this alive.

Tucker leaned in, pressed a kiss on her mouth. He figured it wouldn't help. He was wrong about that, too. It sure helped him, and it was a good reminder of just how much was at stake. Not just his father's and sister's lives.

But Laine's.

He gave her one last look. There was no way he would say goodbye, but Tucker knew in the back of his mind that this could have a very bad ending. He got ready to move, but the moment he leaned out from the tree, he spotted the headlights from a vehicle barreling up the road toward the house.

Colt.

Thank God. His brother must have heard the shots and come to help. Maybe he'd brought the deputy and the ranch hands with him, too, in case the shooter had reinforcements.

The shooter reacted to those headlights, all right. He stopped firing, and Tucker saw him pivot in Colt's direction. Tucker couldn't let him shoot at Colt, so even though he was way out of position, he double tapped the trigger to get the shooter's attention.

It worked.

The person dropped to the ground.

It was exactly the distraction Tucker needed, and it meant he didn't have to leave Laine alone and unguarded behind the trees. He hauled Laine to her feet and got her moving toward his dad's truck.

Tucker tried to keep watch all around them to make sure the shooter didn't have backup planted around the ranch. With the distraction that Buford had created at

Tucker's place, it was possible several gunmen had come undetected onto the ranch. They could be waiting anywhere, ready to ambush them.

Laine and he ran, but they were still yards from the truck when the shots started again. They weren't going toward Colt. They were going toward him and Laine.

Tucker cursed and kept running. It wouldn't do any good to pull Laine back to the ground, since that's where most of the shots were landing. The bullets were kicking up dirt all around them. The truck was off-limits now, too, because the shooter had moved in that direction.

Mercy, he and Laine were trapped.

Tucker just tightened his grip on her and kept running toward his brother's house.

The place looked like a giant skeleton with the moonlight bouncing off the pale wooden frame. The walls were only partially up, but there were plenty of places for him and Laine to take cover. So Tucker ran as if their lives depended on it.

Because they did.

The shots kept coming closer and closer, but missing their mark.

Maybe.

Either this guy was a bad shot, or the bullets were meant to drive them to a specific place.

Not a comforting thought.

That's why Tucker tried to see if there was anyone lurking in the shadows of all that construction. But he saw nothing. So, as soon as he reached the front of the house, he pulled Laine inside.

Just like that, the shots stopped.

Tucker was partly thankful for that. It meant he could

hear anyone trying to sneak up on them. But it also meant the shooter could be coming in pursuit.

Laine and he needed to find better positions.

It'd been more than a week since he'd been to the construction site, and Tucker wasn't familiar with the layout. He glanced around, spotted the stairs that he figured would lead to the yet-to-be-completed second floor. The height would give him a good vantage point from which to spot the shooter and anyone else he'd brought with him.

"This way," he said. Keeping Laine close, he made his way up the stairs. Tucker paused at the top and looked around, but again didn't see anyone.

The walls had been framed on the top floor, and there were gaping holes where the windows would eventually go. It wasn't enough cover for one person, much less two, but he'd been right about the vantage point. He had a bird's-eye view of the surrounding pastures and the house.

Tucker spotted his dad and Rosalie, still cowering where he'd last seen them. Colt was in the front driveway of the main ranch house positioned behind the door of his truck.

No sign of the shooter, though.

But the guy was still nearby because he sent a shot in Colt's direction, pinning his brother down.

Tucker maneuvered Laine behind a stack of lumber and away from the stairs, in case someone tried to get to them from that direction. He inched his way toward the front, still looking for the idiot who'd tried to kill them. It sickened Tucker to think of the guy getting away or hurting Colt, but it sickened him even more that he or one of his cronies could already be in place to strike again.

Tucker hadn't even gotten in place when he heard a strange sound. Not footsteps or gunshots, but almost a groaning noise. His gaze flew to Laine, praying he'd been wrong about the sound coming from her direction.

But he wasn't wrong.

The groaning sound turned to a loud snap. The floor gave way, and Laine called out for Tucker as she fell through the broken wood.

Chapter Seventeen

Everything happened so fast. Much too fast for Laine to do anything to break her fall.

One second she was standing on the second story of Cooper's future house, and the next she was slamming into the floor below her. She landed on her back, and with nothing to break her fall, she had her breath knocked right out of her.

The pain shot through her, and with her lungs clenched, she had to fight just to sit up.

"Laine?" Tucker shouted, and she could hear him running on the floor above.

But Laine also heard something else.

Movement to her right.

Despite the pain, she shifted her attention in that direction and saw something she definitely didn't want to see. The same shadowy figure from the stairs at the McKinnon house.

He took aim at her.

Laine forced herself to move. Not easy to do with every muscle in her body aching, and maybe even a broken bone. Still, she moved. She scrambled behind a partial wall.

Barely in the nick of time.

A bullet came right at her.

The shot smacked into one of the wooden studs, rattling the wall and also rattling her even though the shot itself hardly made a sound. The gunman was now using a silencer. Maybe so that none of the McKinnons would know that she and Tucker were being attacked again.

This couldn't be happening.

Tucker, his family and she were right back in the middle of danger. The only bright spot in it all was that the babies were at the safe house, far away from the bullets. She was thankful that Tucker had had the foresight to get them out of harm's way.

Of course, he wouldn't see it that way.

He'd see it as a failure on his part, since he hadn't been able to protect everyone else. Her included. But she knew the only reason she was alive at all was because of Tucker.

"Laine?" Tucker shouted again.

She could tell he was at the top of the unfinished stairs. No railing. Just bare steps that jutted up to the opening that would become the landing. The shooter obviously could tell where Tucker was, too, because the next shot swished in his direction.

Laine nearly shouted for him to stay down, but she didn't want to risk him answering, since it was clear the shooter was gunning for him.

She tested her legs, and even though she had cuts and bruises, there didn't seem to be any broken bones, so she started moving. She inched her way along the partial wall, trying not to make a sound.

Above her, she heard Tucker moving again. At least she prayed it was Tucker. This monster could have brought more killers with him, and it was possible he had them close enough to go after Tucker again.

Still listening for any movement from their attacker, Laine reached the end of the wall, and she peered up at the gaping hole above her. It was the edge of the stair-well, and she could just make out Tucker. He had his gun aimed and his foot positioned as if he were about to make his way downstairs.

Laine shook her head, hoping he'd see her. She didn't want him walking directly toward a killer, and she was certain he was nearby, ready to strike.

But Tucker didn't stay put.

He paused when he landed on the first step. Paused again as he made his way down.

He was on the third step when the shot zinged through the air.

Even though the gunman was still using a silencer, there was no mistaking that the shooter had been aim-ing at Tucker, because the bullet bashed into the drywall right next to him, sending powdery dust raining down on her. Since she was dragging in air through her mouth, she dragged that in, too, and had to choke back a cough.

Two more shots came at Tucker. Then in the blink of an eye, the shooter's direction changed.

The bullets started coming at her.

They went right through the drywall. Right at her. Laine was forced to scramble deeper into the house so she wouldn't be hit.

There was no light in this part of the structure because of the exterior wall and floor above, so she crashed into some tools. The clanging noise was practically deafening.

But not loud enough for Laine to miss the sound of footsteps.

These weren't coming from the stairs where she'd last seen Tucker. They were coming from behind her.

Laine didn't bolt, though she had to hold herself back from doing just that. It was too dark for her to see much of anything, and if she ran, she could land right in the arms of a killer.

She felt around on the floor and located a screwdriver from the toppled tool case. It wasn't much of a weapon, but it was better than nothing. So was the long nail she snatched up. Holding the screwdriver like a knife, Laine eased up a little, trying to sort through the murky shadows and spot the killer.

Nothing.

No footsteps, either, though it was hard to hear with her own heartbeat crashing in her ears.

"Laine?" Tucker said again.

It wasn't a shout, but rather a whisper. She couldn't pinpoint his exact position, but it sounded as if he was still near the stairs. It definitely hadn't been Tucker's footsteps that she'd heard earlier.

And that meant their attacker had moved closer.

Laine tried not to make a sound. Hard to do, though, since she was breathing through her mouth. She clamped her teeth over her bottom lip, prayed and glanced around, looking for the monster who'd put them in the middle of this nightmare.

Another sound.

More footsteps.

Definitely coming from the stairs. Either their attacker was going after Tucker or Tucker was trying to make his way downstairs to her.

Again, she nearly called out to warn him not to do anything that could get him killed, but the debate came to a crashing halt when she heard the next sound.

It was close.

Too close.

She reeled around, prepared to use the screwdriver to defend herself, but she didn't get the chance. Someone from behind her knocked the screwdriver from her hand, hooked an arm around her neck and dragged her to her feet.

Laine wasn't able to fight off the attack before she felt the barrel of a gun against her head.

TUCKER HEARD LAINE'S GASP, and he figured that wasn't a good sign.

With his gun ready, he inched down the stairs. His instincts were yelling for him to get to her—fast—but it wouldn't help either of them for him to go charging into a situation that could get them both killed.

He reached the bottom step, his gaze slashing from one side of the building to the other. No sign of the shooter or Laine. But he could hear her.

Quick jolts of breath.

She was obviously terrified, and that got him hurrying. Tucker had to get to her.

With his shooting wrist bracketed with his hand, he moved to the left side of the stairs, keeping cover behind a stack of building materials. Tucker's heart went to the floor. He'd found Laine all right, and she was alive.

For now.

But she might not be for long if Tucker didn't do something. The dirtwad holding a gun to her head could pull the trigger and kill her with one shot.

"Let her go," Tucker ordered. He couldn't see the person because of the spotty darkness, but he was pretty sure it was a man.

Maybe Hague or Darren.

However, it could also be just another hired gun like Buford. If so, then Rhonda could be calling the shots—literally.

Tucker inched closer but stopped when the person jammed the gun harder against Laine's head. He had no trouble seeing her face. The ghost-white moon seemed to land on her like a spotlight, and he could see the absolute terror in her eyes.

He could also see something else.

She wasn't surrendering. No, there was plenty of fight left in her body, and that could be a bad thing. He didn't want her fighting back.

Not now, anyway.

After all, if this creep had wanted her dead, he would have already shot her. Tucker, too. And he hadn't fired a shot. That meant he wanted something from both of them, and Tucker got a good idea of what that was when the man started to drag her back, deeper into the shadows.

He was kidnapping Laine.

"Stop," Tucker warned him. He tested his theory that this guy wanted him alive by taking one step out from cover. He could always dive back if the creep fired.

But he didn't.

"What do you want with us?" Tucker demanded.

Silence.

The guy just kept moving, although Laine wasn't exactly cooperating. She was struggling. Well, she was until the guy whispered something in her ear. That stopped her. She practically froze. And there was probably only one reason for her to do that.

Her attacker had threatened to shoot Tucker.

And he might try. But Tucker didn't have any plans

for Laine and him to die tonight. Or for Laine to be kidnapped by this trigger-happy nut job.

He hadn't seen any unusual vehicles parked around the house or the ranch, but that didn't mean this man didn't have a car stashed somewhere. If he managed to get Laine away from there, God knew what he would do to her.

"You know I'm not just going to let you take her," Tucker said, moving right along with them. "Just tell me what you want, and we can settle this right here, right now."

Still nothing.

Hard to bargain with the devil when he didn't know what the devil wanted. Of course, as long as he stayed quiet, Tucker didn't know who he was dealing with. It could be either Darren or Hague, trying to conceal their identity.

So far, it was working.

The man dragged her toward one of the spaces where the windows would soon be. Right now, they were just giant holes, with plenty of space for someone to slip through. And that was obviously the plan, because while keeping a firm grip on Laine, he ducked down a little.

Just enough for the moonlight to glint across his face. *Martin Hague.*

Tucker cursed. Hague wouldn't exactly have been a formidable foe, *if* he hadn't been armed. But that gun was the ultimate equalizer. Desperation, too. Tucker was betting Hague must have been desperate to come to the McKinnon ranch and pull a stunt like this.

"He told me he wouldn't hurt you if I go with him," Laine said.

"Yeah, right," Tucker mumbled. "I'm thinking Hague's not a credible source when it comes to a comment like that."

Judging from Laine's expression, she wasn't buying it, either, but she didn't exactly have a lot of options. She wasn't armed, and even though Hague wasn't a hulking brute like Buford, he was still bigger and stronger than her.

"Buford's dead," Tucker told Hague, just in case he didn't know.

But obviously he did. There was still enough moonlight for Tucker to see that Hague didn't even react to that. Too bad. Tucker had hoped it would shake him up enough to make a mistake. Any mistake.

All Tucker needed was one clean shot.

"You killed Buford," Tucker concluded. "He was your own hired gun, and you made sure he was dead."

Hague didn't confirm or deny that. He just kept moving. A few more steps and he'd be at the window. If Tucker couldn't talk him out of this before then, he'd have to take drastic measures.

Anything to stop Hague from leaving with Laine.

"I'm figuring you told Buford to set the explosives," Tucker went on, hoping anything he said would slow the guy down or distract him. "They were small enough for him to have carried them in his pocket when he was running from the deputy and into my house. But he didn't know you'd already given him poison that would kill him."

Again, Hague didn't confirm it. Not verbally, anyway. But he clearly wasn't surprised by anything Tucker had said.

"What was Buford going to do—blackmail you or something?" Tucker asked. "Or maybe you were worried about that plea deal he tried to make before all hell broke loose."

"Maybe," Hague mumbled.

Since it was the first thing Hague had said to him since the whole ordeal had started, Tucker figured he'd hit a nerve. He took another swing at it.

"When you deal with criminals, it shouldn't surprise you when one tries to backstab you. You hired Buford, Hines and the other gunmen. So what happened? Did Buford want more money from you to keep his mouth shut and to take the plea deal off the table?"

"Don't know why you'd care," Hague snarled.

"I care because I'm wearing a badge. And because you're holding an innocent woman at gunpoint."

"She's not innocent!" Another nerve.

But Tucker didn't like the result of this one that he'd managed to hit.

"She started all of this by sticking her nose where it didn't belong," Hague grumbled. "She should have never shown up at the baby farm."

True, but if she hadn't, the twins might not have been rescued. Of course, Laine was paying a high price for saving them, and Tucker didn't doubt that she'd pay the ultimate price if it came down to it. There were a lot of lawmen who weren't as brave as she was.

Hague's grip tightened on Laine's neck, and he dug the gun deeper into her temple. She made a sound of pain that she clearly tried to bite back. No doubt so it wouldn't send Tucker into a rage. He wanted to think he wouldn't do that, but it was Laine at the end of that gun barrel.

Laine made another small sound when Hague jerked

her back, putting her in a choke hold. Tucker heard the sound of pain loud and clear, and it ate away at him. Hell. He couldn't let Hague keep hurting her like this.

"Laine isn't the reason your baby farm was closed down," Tucker went on, though he figured it wouldn't do any good. Still, he had to try. "You were breaking the law, and she was only doing her job."

"She got in the way," Hague fired back. "And now I'll use her to fix what she messed up."

That put some ice in his blood. "Use her how?"

"You'll soon find out." Hague lifted his left leg and put it through the window slot. "I'll be in touch with the ransom demand."

"What ransom?" Tucker snapped.

"The one you'll pay if you want to get her back alive."

Part of him wanted to believe this was for real, that Hague had no plans to kill them, that he could be appeased with just money. But Tucker couldn't see how that would happen. Both Laine and he were loose ends, and even though he didn't know Hague's plan, he wouldn't want to leave witnesses like them behind.

"Tell your brother and any of the others to back off," Hague warned him. "If they don't, I'll hurt Laine."

Tucker hadn't actually seen Colt, but he figured now that his brother wasn't being pinned down by gunfire that Colt would quickly make his way to Cooper's house. Maybe Hague had figured that, too. Most of the ranch hands, however, would probably stay at the main house to guard Roy and Rosalie.

"Tell them!" Hague repeated, shouting this time. Mercy, the man was quickly losing control of his icy composure.

Not good.

Because in a fit of temper, Hague could start a gun-fight that would get Laine killed.

"Colt, hold your fire," Tucker called out.

Maybe his brother was close enough to hear him, and if he was, perhaps Colt would indeed hold his fire, unless he had the perfect kill shot aimed at Hague. That wouldn't be easy with the darkness and with Hague gripping Laine so close to him. Still, it could happen, and Tucker had to hold on to that thought like a lifeline.

"I'm sorry," Laine said, and Tucker knew she was talking to him.

He gave her his best flat bad-boy look to let her know an apology would just piss him off. But the look fell short when he saw her moving her left hand.

And Tucker saw what she was holding.

A nail.

Laine gave him a slight nod, and he knew then that she was about to do something that was a thousand steps past being dangerous.

"No," Tucker mumbled.

But it was too late.

Tucker saw Laine draw back her hand and jam the nail into the side of Hague's thigh. Before the man could even react—or pull the trigger—Tucker did the only thing he could do.

He launched himself at Hague and prayed he would be able to stop him in time.

Chapter Eighteen

It was all a blur of sounds and movements for Laine.

Hague howled in pain, cursing her in the same breath, and she felt his hand tense on the gun. Laine braced herself for him to pull the trigger.

But he didn't get the chance to do that.

Hague was already off balance with his one leg out the window opening, but his precarious position got significantly worse when Tucker rammed full force into them.

The pain was instant, like an explosion going off inside her head, and it took Laine a moment to realize the pain wasn't from a bullet but rather from being bashed into the wall. Hague jerked her back, using her to break his fall, and the side of her head slammed into the wooden frame.

Before she could react or even catch her breath, she felt herself falling right along with Hague, and all three of them landed on the ground just outside the window.

She was trapped between them.

Worse, Hague still had his gun. It was jamming into her neck, and if he pulled the trigger, she'd be dead.

Laine tried to do something about that.

No way did she want to just lie there while Hague killed both her and Tucker.

She had somehow managed to keep a grip on the nail

so she thrust it at Hague again. His shout of pain was almost deafening since his mouth was right against her ear. Obviously, she'd done some damage, but it only seemed to enrage him even more. It certainly didn't slow the man down, and he was fighting like a wildcat, using her body as a shield to keep Tucker from attacking him.

Tucker wasn't exactly his usual calm self, either. He was cursing Hague and fighting, too, trying to push Laine out of the way so he could get to the man. The only thing she could do was try to stay out of their way in case Tucker got the chance to pound Hague to dust.

Hague shifted his gun away from her neck. Aiming it right at Tucker. Her heart jumped to her throat, and Laine hit him with the nail again.

And again.

She would have hit him a dozen times if he hadn't hit her. Cursing, Hague latched onto her hair with his left hand and yanked it back so hard that she was the one yelping in pain.

It only made Tucker fight harder.

She saw Tucker's fist come right at her. Except it wasn't coming at her, but rather at Hague's jaw. Tucker connected, and Hague's head flopped back for an instant. It was just enough for him to let go of her hair so she could stab him with the nail again. This time she went after his neck, hoping to hit an artery.

But she didn't.

Hague moved at the last second, and the nail glanced off his shoulder.

He didn't even seem to react to the new wound, though Laine was certain she'd drawn more blood. Probably because the adrenaline was fueling him. It was fueling her, too, but Hague was still stronger than she was, and he dragged her back in front of him. He then bashed his gun against her hand so hard that the nail went flying.

Laine was ready to drop down so she could hopefully give Tucker enough room to fire. But Hague put her back in a choke hold, even tighter than the one before. If this kept up, she'd soon lose consciousness. Or worse. He'd crush her windpipe and kill her. She had to do something.

But what?

She was fighting as hard as she could, and Hague was holding Tucker at bay by keeping the gun to her head.

Without warning, a shot cracked through the air.

Laine screamed and tried to get to Tucker. She was positive that Hague had shot him, but the bullet hadn't come from Hague's gun.

It'd come from the front of the house.

Maybe from Colt, or from one of the ranch hands. Laine prayed it hadn't been fired by one of Hague's henchmen. At least it hadn't been Buford, because according to Tucker, that particular killer was already dead. Still, Hague might have others out there helping him.

"If you want her dead, go ahead and fire another shot," Hague shouted. He had complete control of her again. She was positioned in front of him, the gun digging into the back of her head.

"Hold your fire," Tucker said to whoever was out there. Whoever it was, maybe he could get into a position to shoot Hague since the angle was all wrong for Tucker.

Hague waited a moment, his heartbeat thudding against her back and his breath gusting in her ear. He had the smell of fear, blood and sweat all over him. She'd lost count of how many times she'd struck him with that nail or how many times Tucker had punched him, but

from the corner of her eye, she could see the blood trick-
ling down his face.

"Now drop your gun and get on the ground," Hague
ordered Tucker.

Tucker shook his head. "I can't let you take her, and
that's exactly what you'll do if I'm not armed and ready
to stop you."

"You don't have a choice. You already know I'll do
anything to put an end to this. Anything, including pulling the trigger that'll kill her."

Again, Tucker shook his head. "It doesn't have to be
this way. We can work something out."

Laine didn't know how Tucker managed it, but he kept
his voice calm. She'd heard that tone before, when she
had been on the scene and he'd had to negotiate with a
parent who'd taken his own child hostage. Tucker had
managed to save the child, and she prayed he could do
the same thing now.

Unless her staying alive would somehow endanger the
twins. Was that it?

That put her heart right in her throat.

"This is about the babies," she said. "You're going to
exchange them for me. Except we both know you aren't
going to let me live."

That earned her another hard jab from his gun. "I told
you to put down your weapon," Hague repeated to Tucker.

And he moved the gun to her already injured arm.

"I'll put a bullet in her," Hague threatened. "It won't
kill her, but I wonder just how long you'll be able to stand
there with her screaming in pain."

Laine tried to brace herself for the shot. She doubted
she could stay quiet if Hague carried through with

that threat, but she hated that he would use her pain to manipulate Tucker.

The muscles in Tucker's jaw stirred. "If you hurt her again, you die."

"If you don't put down your gun, I'll hurt her," Hague countered.

They stood there glaring at each other, and she saw the moment that Tucker surrendered to the demand. Without taking his eyes off Hague, he stooped down and eased the gun onto the ground just inches from his own boots.

"I can't watch while he hurts you," Tucker said, his voice barely a whisper.

He sounded plenty sorry about that. And he probably was. This was personal for him now, and she could blame their lovemaking for that. He'd lost his objectivity, and it was now playing into how he was handling this.

It was playing into how she was handling it, too.

If Hague killed her, at least it'd be fast, but she would die a thousand times over if he turned that gun on Tucker. Thankfully, Hague seemed to want her.

"If it's really just the money you want," Laine offered the monster with the gun to her head, "I can get it for you."

"Oh, you will," Hague assured her. "Tucker will, too. I need all that you two have and a lot more. Now, stand up," Hague ordered Tucker. "And keep your hands where I can see them."

Tucker stayed stooped down, his hand near his gun where he could hopefully snatch it up if necessary. "If you owned the baby farm, why are you being pressured for money?"

"Stand up!" Hague shouted.

Cursing, Tucker had no choice but to do just that.

Hague started inching her backward. Away from Tucker and the house. Also away from Colt or whoever had fired that shot. Laine hoped there was some way someone could sneak up behind Hague, but unfortunately, there was only open space around them since Cooper's house was being built on the edge of the pasture.

"Let me guess," Tucker went on, glaring at Hague. "You borrowed money from the wrong people to fund this sick operation of yours."

"Why do you care?" Hague snapped, still moving.

"I'd just like to know the reason you're planning to demand a ransom." Tucker lifted his shoulder. "That, and I'm puzzled about something that Buford said right before he died."

Hague froze. It was the first time she'd felt him that still since the attack had started. "What the hell did he say?" Hague snapped.

Tucker lifted his shoulder again, as if this were the most mundane subject. It obviously wasn't, and Laine had no idea if Tucker was bluffing or if Buford had indeed managed to say something incriminating.

"Buford said he had some info stashed away in a safe-deposit box. Said it would prove it was you working the baby farm." Tucker paused. "I'm pretty sure Buford figured out you poisoned him. I'm also sure he didn't trust you any more than you trusted him."

Because Hague was so close to her, she felt the change in his breathing, and even though she hadn't thought it possible, his muscles tensed even more.

Obviously, this was a glitch he hadn't expected.

"You're lying," Hague said.

"Don't have to. Buford was almost dead when I got to him, but trust me, almost dead men can do plenty of talking. Especially since he wanted his killer to pay for poisoning him."

Hague stayed quiet a moment, his breath gusting even harder. "What safe-deposit box? Where is it?"

Tucker shook his head. "Didn't say. But I'm thinking it won't be hard to find once my brother gets the search warrants. Oh, wait. Were you planning on involving my brothers and the Marshals' service in this?"

Clearly, that was the last thing Hague wanted, and his profanity proved that. He'd likely wanted to make a clean getaway, and then he could use her to get money from her own family and from Tucker.

And then he would murder them.

Hard to kill dozens of people who could come in contact with what might be in a safe-deposit box.

"If Buford left any kind of evidence, and that's a huge *if*," Hague said, "then my advice is for you to leave it hidden away. There's someone other than me who'd kill to keep all of this under wraps."

Laine tried to figure out if that was a lie, but there was no indication that it was anything but the truth. Worse, it made sense for someone else to have been involved in the baby farm operation.

With his bombshell dropped, Hague got her moving again.

"Who'll try to kill us?" Tucker pressed.

Hague laughed, but there was absolutely no humor in it. "Just giving you his name would be bad for all of us. He plays dirty, and if I don't turn over Dawn's babies to him, a lot of people will die. Myself included. He's the one who put the hit on her—not me—when he didn't get the twins he'd been guaranteed. But even if he hadn't wanted her dead, I couldn't allow her to stay alive. She could have spilled details about the baby farm."

That put some more fire in Tucker's eyes. His mouth tightened. "This piece of dirt you're talking about paid for the babies?"

"Hey, I run a business, not a charity."

"You *ran* a business," Tucker said, his teeth coming together. "That's about to end. And there's no way in hell I'm letting you give those babies to the person who ordered a hit on their mother."

"You don't have a say in the matter, McKinnon. Ditto for giving me whatever amount of cash I demand. No say whatsoever. Without the money, you don't get Laine back, and even a fool can see you'd do anything to stop her from being hurt."

"You're wrong," Laine insisted. "There's too much bad blood between Tucker and me. He's just doing his job here, but he'd sacrifice me in a second if it meant taking you down."

Tucker didn't argue. In fact, he didn't say a word. He just kept that fierce glare nailed to Hague.

In the distance, she heard a slight whistle and remembered that Colt had made that same sound when he'd gone into the woods looking for Buford after he'd tried to kidnap her. Tucker must have heard it, too, but he didn't react.

Hague did, though.

He looked in the direction of the sound. Just a simple movement of his head. The moment seemed to freeze, but Laine could almost feel the attack before it happened.

With Hague distracted, Tucker scooped up his gun and charged toward them. Laine did her part and prayed it was the right thing to do.

She fell backward, throwing all of her weight into Hague and hoping to topple him.

Maybe because he was already distracted, Hague clearly hadn't expected it, and she felt herself falling again. Hague latched onto her, and in the same motion, he slammed the butt of the gun against her face. Laine could have sworn that she saw stars, and it knocked her to the ground.

Hague went after her again, clawing at her and trying to put her back in front of him.

Tucker came at them, not saying a word, but she could feel the rage in him. He dropped down onto his knees and punched Hague full force with his fist.

And he just kept on punching.

His fists flew along with the profanity that left his mouth, and Hague could do nothing but drop the gun and let go of her.

"Don't kill him," Laine managed to say. Not because she wanted this piece of slime to live but because she didn't want Tucker to have to deal with the aftermath of killing an unarmed man. He was too good of a lawman for that.

Tucker landed one last punch and moved back just as Colt and two ranch hands rushed up. The three took aim at Hague, but it was clear the man wasn't going anywhere. He could barely move.

"You okay?" Colt asked, volleying glances at Tucker and her.

Tucker nodded but cursed again when his attention landed on her face. Laine felt it then, the trickle of blood on her cheek from where Hague had hit her with the gun. Tucker uttered a single word of really bad profanity, and she caught onto him to stop him from launching himself at Hague again.

"I'm fine," she lied.

She would have said anything at that point to put an end to this, but the truth was her legs were shaking so hard she thought she might collapse.

Tucker solved that problem for her. He slipped his arm around her, supporting her weight, and they started back toward the main house.

"Take this snake to jail," Tucker told his brother.

"Gladly. Maybe he'll even resist arrest so I can add some bruises to his face. It takes some kind of jerk to hit a woman."

Laine was glad Colt hadn't qualified that with *"any woman."* Even one his family considered an enemy. That was indeed progress when it came to the McKinnons.

"I'll call the doctor," Tucker whispered to her. "How bad are you hurt?"

"Not as bad I could have been. Thanks." She tried to brush a kiss on his cheek, but the emotions were still too raw, as if it hurt him to see her, to touch her.

"You need to find Steve Wilkey," Hague shouted back to them.

Laine stopped and shook her head. The name was only vaguely familiar, and it took her a few seconds to realize where she'd heard it before.

"You mean the lawyer you brought to the sheriff's office?" she asked.

"He's a lawyer, all right, but he's not mine." Hague winced and cursed when Colt dragged him to his feet. "He insisted on coming with me because he was sure I'd screwed things up. You're lucky he didn't have all of you killed that day, because those were his hired guns who shot at you."

Despite the steamy heat, that sent an icy chill through her. She wanted to believe that Hague was lying, that there was no other person involved in this. But it didn't sound like a lie.

Tucker turned and faced Hague, but he kept a gentle grip on her. "You owe this man money?"

"Yeah. Plenty of it. Find him and arrest him, because he'll send someone after me even if I'm behind bars. At best, he'll kill me. Or else he'll make me wish he had."

"And why should I be concerned about that?" Tucker fired back. Laine wanted to ask him the same thing. After everything he'd done, she didn't care an ounce what happened to Hague.

"You should be concerned, because Wilkey's after the twins."

Laine was sure her heart skipped a beat or two. Tucker and she exchanged glances, and she prayed he would have some reassurance that it wasn't true. But he only looked as thunderstruck as she felt.

"What'd you mean?" Tucker demanded.

"He has a buyer for the twins," Hague fired back. "A big buyer. Wilkey has men out looking for them now, and there'll be a huge payout for whoever finds them. With Wilkey's resources, if I were you, I'd hurry. Maybe you can get to them before he does.

"Maybe," Hague repeated, his voice and the threat echoing in the darkness.

Chapter Nineteen

Once again, Tucker was watching a medic tend to Laine. This time, they weren't at the sheriff's office but rather in his family's home.

That cut and god-awful bruise that Hague had put on her face turned his stomach. So did the still-haunted look in her eyes. But he knew that look wasn't just from the pain of the attack or the thorough job the medic was doing of cleaning the wound.

No. It was from a different kind of pain and fear.

For the babies.

Tucker was right there on the same page with her. No way could he stand the thought of someone taking those children. Somehow they had to stop this Steve Wilkey from getting close to them.

Or close to Laine, for that matter.

Tucker had already beefed up security at the ranch. The hands were all armed and were patrolling the grounds in case Wilkey came their way. He'd also spoken to Sergeant Egan Caldwell and had learned that Wilkey and his henchmen hadn't come to the safe house.

Thank God.

Tucker hadn't wanted to move the twins. Instead, he

had sent out several Texas Rangers to look for the lawyer and haul him in for questioning.

Hague could have been lying about Wilkey's involvement, but Tucker wanted no stone left unturned when it came to Laine's and the babies' safety.

They'd gotten somewhat lucky tonight. Everyone was alive, and his dad and Rosalie were all in one piece. Thankfully, none of them had tried to play hero and come storming into Cooper's house, where Hague had been holding Laine at gunpoint. Roy and his twin sister had stayed put on Colt's order, and instead of injuries—like Laine's—all they would have to deal with were the horrible memories of the attack.

That was more than enough, and was likely the reason Rosalie had gone back to the guesthouse as soon as Hague had been taken away. She'd already been through so much with the kidnapping of her own baby that this could have brought it all back to the surface. He made a mental note to check on her.

Once he'd seen to Laine, that is.

"I think she'll be fine," his dad said to him. Again. Roy could no doubt tell that this had shaken him to the core, but it was a surprise that his dad and Colt were being so, well, friendly.

They certainly weren't giving Laine any signals that they wanted her immediately out of there. And that was good. It was a start, anyway. Because after everything that'd gone on tonight, Tucker couldn't see himself giving Laine the heave-ho.

Maybe they could even date or something.

Images of her naked flashed through his head. Okay, so they were well past the dating stage, but he had no intention of letting this go back to where it'd been a few days before. The trouble was he didn't know how to go about making sure that she stayed in his life.

"You're staring at me again," Laine mumbled, turning away from him. "I must look pretty bad for you to keep doing that."

"You look amazing," Tucker blurted out, catching both his father's and Colt's attention despite the fact that Colt was on the phone talking to Reed, who had Hague in custody at the jail.

The corner of Laine's mouth lifted for just a brief moment, but it didn't take more than a couple of seconds for her to get that haunted look again. Tears came, too, and then nothing in the world could keep Tucker from her side. He didn't elbow the medic aside. Not exactly, anyway. But he put himself between the guy and her so he could pull Laine into his arms.

"We can't let that man get to the babies," she whispered, and the tears came streaking down her bruised cheek. Tucker tried to gently kiss them away. They just kept coming. All he could do was stand there and let her get it all out.

"We won't," he assured her.

He led her to the other side of the room. It wasn't exactly private, but it was better than the center of the foyer. The medic looked at them as if he might come over and resume whatever he'd been doing, but Tucker waved him off.

"Egan's a good man," Tucker added, trying to soothe Laine. "No way would he let anyone get to the twins. Jack and Jill," Tucker added because he thought they could use some levity.

It worked a little. Laine tried to smile anyway.

Roy groaned softly, shook his head. "You gotta come

up with better names than that, especially since Laine said she was planning to adopt them."

"I am." That helped, too, and she brought her chin a little higher. "Any ideas?"

Now it was Tucker who groaned. If Rosalie had been in the room, at least there would have been some possibly good input, but he wasn't expecting much from his dad and brother.

And he didn't get much, either.

"Frick and Frack," Colt suggested. "Or maybe Trouble One and Trouble Two?"

Laine winced, but there was actually a little lightness beneath it.

"Laine, I always thought your grandmother had a pretty name," Roy spoke up. "Mattie. She was a fine woman. Good heart."

It was the first time in twenty-three years Tucker had heard anyone say a kind word about the Braddocks. But his dad was right. Tucker remembered Laine's paternal grandmother, and even though she'd long since passed away, she deserved a namesake.

Laine nodded. "Mattie it is." And she swallowed hard, as if she had a sudden lump in her throat.

Tucker didn't dare suggest using her father's name for the boy. Too much pain there yet, especially with the renewed memories from the upcoming trial.

"Matt goes pretty good with Mattie," he offered.

Another nod, and this time she gave a little smile. "I like it. Thanks." She mumbled the same to Roy and gave Colt a mock scolding glance, which he probably didn't even see because he got another call from Reed. Colt stepped away to take it.

The moment didn't last long, and Tucker saw the fear

creep back into Laine's eyes. Before he could start another round of reassurance, or distraction, his phone rang. Not Egan, thank God, with news that they'd had a *visitor* at the safe house. It was another Ranger, Griffin Morris.

"We found Steve Wilkey," Griffin said the moment Tucker answered. "I'm pretty sure your prisoner, Hague, was telling the truth about this jerk funding the baby farm. I pulled up his rap sheet on the way to his house, and he's corrupt all the way to the bone. He's been disbarred for years now and always seems to be one step ahead of the law."

Tucker had been doing a lot of cursing lately, but he added some more. "Why didn't Wilkey show up on the radar before now?"

"Maybe because his only association with the baby farm was through Hague."

That was possible. Heck, Hague hadn't even been on their radar until he'd shown up and tried to take the twins.

"What's Wilkey saying about all of this?" Tucker went on.

"He's not saying much of anything. We showed up at his house, and it didn't have a pretty ending. Before we could even tell him why we were there, he turned two goons on us. They shot at us, and we had to return fire."

Hell. Wilkey was obviously a violent man and had been there with Laine at the sheriff's office. Just a few feet away from her. And Tucker had been so focused on their other suspects, he hadn't realized they had a second snake in their midst.

"Wilkey joined the gunfight," Griffin went on, "and he and both of his men are dead."

The relief was overwhelming. Wilkey and his henchmen couldn't go after the babies now. But it would have been nice to get some answers from one of them so they could tie this up into a neat little package. Maybe he could get those answers from Colt after he finished his call with Reed.

"While he was shooting at us, Wilkey yelled out that he was going to kill Hague for setting us on him," the Ranger continued. "That's why I figured any part he had in the baby farm was only between Hague and him. Wilkey didn't name anyone else, and he was sure doing a lot of yelling."

"Yeah. Hague said that Wilkey had a buyer for the twins so maybe he'd already paid Hague and wanted him to deliver on the goods."

A sickening thought. Hague and Wilkey had treated the babies like livestock, ready to be sold to the highest bidder, and Tucker didn't even want to go with the rest of that thought. God knew what the highest bidder actually wanted with the twins. He figured if they'd been loving parents without police records, they would have taken a more normal route to adoption.

"I've already had someone call Egan to tell him the danger's passed," Griffin added. "The safe house is just five miles or so from you. Figured you'd want the babies brought back to you ASAP. Unless you want them to go to social services. If so, I can call Egan back."

"No." Tucker didn't even have to think about it. "I want them brought here to the ranch. The woman who's adopting them will take custody."

That would be possible now that there were no other obstacles in her way. No one in Dawn's or Laverty's family to stop her petition to get custody of Mattie and Matt. With Laine's position in the community, it appeared to be smooth sailing, despite her being a single mom.

"Oh, and tell Egan to hurry," Tucker added to Griffin. "We're anxious to see them." It would help Laine to be with them and hold them.

Heck, it'd help him, too.

When he finished the call, he could tell that Laine had heard every word of the conversation because she smiled and nearly launched herself into his arms. The medic must have decided he didn't want to be part of the little celebration because he packed up his things.

"Her injuries aren't that serious," the medic said to no one in particular. "She should make an appointment with her doctor, though."

Tucker assured him that would happen. And it would. Laine would get a thorough checkup. After they'd celebrated a little, that is.

The medic mumbled something about needing to get back to the hospital, and he let himself out.

"They're safe. We're safe," Laine said. She kissed him, and Tucker realized it helped his raw nerves and spent adrenaline hugely.

However, they still had an audience.

Something that Tucker didn't remember until he heard his dad clear his throat. He broke the kiss, fully expecting Roy to give him a look or some kind of reminder that this wasn't a good thing.

That didn't happen.

Roy reached out and gave Tucker's arm a pat. The sort of pat a man gave his son when he was proud of him.

But he couldn't be proud.

Could he?

"You won't hear any complaints from me," his dad offered. "Or from the rest of the family, if I have a say in it."

And then he did something else that surprised the heck

out of Tucker. Roy leaned in and brushed a kiss on Laine's cheek. The unbruised one. If there was any trace of that bad blood, it didn't show now.

Tucker was still in a bit of shock. He didn't notice that Colt had finished his call and was staring at them as if he couldn't figure out what to make of it.

Then his brother shrugged. "I guess I won't complain, either. Well, not much, anyway."

Laine smiled, nodded. "I'll try not to make a nuisance of myself."

Tucker frowned. He sure didn't like the sound of that, but before he could voice it, Colt pointed to his phone, reminding him that there were some darn important ends to tie up.

"Hague's cooperating big-time with Reed. Yakking his head off in the hopes of getting a plea deal."

"He's not getting one," Tucker argued.

At the same moment Laine said, "Not a chance. I want him in prison for life."

"That's the plan. Reed told him the same thing, but he's talking anyway. Hague said he convinced Dawn and Rhonda that Darren was the bad guy. That's why they were afraid of him."

Well, that explained some things. Not all, though.

"But what about the recording Darren had?" Tucker asked. "Dawn used the word *she*. Does that mean she was afraid of Rhonda, too?"

"Probably. Hague wouldn't have wanted the women to be too chummy, because they might put one and one together and figure he was in charge of the baby farm. If he'd lie about Darren being bad, I don't see why he wouldn't lie about Rhonda, too."

True. And while it was good that Darren hadn't done

anything wrong, Tucker wouldn't have minded a few minor charges thrown at him.

Okay, that was the jealousy talking.

He wasn't just riled that Laine was avoiding making a *nuisance* of herself, but he was also irritated that she'd once been in love with that selfish rat who'd treated her like dirt. Laine wasn't Darren's. She was his.

Whoa.

That brought him skidding to a mental halt.

Laine wasn't his and hadn't been since they were kids. Though he was pretty sure he wanted her to be. He was also sure he wanted a lot more than a kiss from her in his granddaddy's kitchen.

"Could you excuse us a moment?" he said to his dad and brother, leading Laine out onto the porch.

Even though there were plenty of ranch hands still milling around, it was a better place from which to watch for the babies. It was also a better place for him to make a fool out of himself with what he wanted to say.

Tucker wasn't exactly sure of the words. They might not even have made sense, but he knew he couldn't let Laine leave with Mattie and Matt.

"Look, I know I'm not exactly daddy material, but I was serious about my offer to help you raise them."

It was a start, but judging from the way the corners of her mouth turned down, it wasn't the exact offer she wanted to hear.

"Or not," he said, testing it. That didn't test well at all, and Tucker found himself frowning. It was obvious he needed to say something, but he wasn't quite sure what that was.

She huffed, and her hand went on her hip. "For Pete's

sake, we've been through this, and you already need a reminder."

"Yeah, I guess I do." He didn't want to make an ass out of himself and assume that Laine was asking for a whole lot more than just a commitment to help with the babies.

"When was your last real kiss?" she asked.

Oh. Tucker knew exactly what to do with that question.

He eased her to him and kissed her. It was long, hard and pretty darn satisfying. Well, until oxygen became an issue. "That one."

She made a dreamy little sound of pleasure before she pulled back her shoulders and stared at him. "Well, at least you're better with your mouth than you are with your words. Have you ever told a woman you love her?"

Tucker had to shake his head. He'd had women in his life, but he'd never wanted to lie to them. And saying "I love you" would definitely have been a lie.

Until now, he realized.

The corner of her mouth kicked up as if she knew she'd just hit pay dirt. Probably because he had a goofy look on his face. Hard to keep his cocky bad-boy look when he'd just figured out what exactly was going on in his head.

And in his heart.

She wadded up a handful of his shirt and pulled him back to her. "Here's the deal," Laine said, her mouth against his. "I'm in love with you. Always have been, always will be. Yes, I want your help raising the twins, but I want more than just that."

Laine paused, kissed him. "Tucker McKinnon, I want it all. I want *you*."

Well, heck. More pay dirt. Tucker figured he should just keep quiet since she was saying all the things that he wanted her to say. All the things he wanted to hear.

"You're in love with me?" he asked, just to make sure he hadn't misheard her. And because he wanted to hear her say it again.

"Yes. Of course I love you." Her smile got even wider. He had to have a sample of it to see if it tasted as good as it looked on her.

It did.

Like his birthday and Christmas all rolled into one.

She pulled back, obviously waiting, and Tucker wanted to say to her what he already knew in his heart. But before he could do that, he saw the approaching headlights of a vehicle making its way up the road.

Because of the nightmare they'd just gone through, Tucker automatically stepped in front of Laine and reached for his gun. But it was a false alarm.

The best kind.

It was Egan in an SUV, and he was no doubt bringing the babies home. Tucker and Laine made it all the way down the steps before Tucker decided that this was indeed their home.

Well, hopefully.

He might have to convince Laine of that first.

Tucker let her make it to the SUV ahead of him, and the nanny bodyguard stepped out. She handed one of the babies to a waiting and eager Laine. Since the baby was dressed in a blue gown, he figured it was Matt.

He was glad they'd taken the time to come up with better names.

Laine pressed a flurry of kisses on the baby's sleeping face and then handed him to Tucker so she could do the same to Mattie. Heck, he hadn't thought it possible, but they were cuter than they had been a few hours before when they'd left for the safe house.

Since Tucker figured this kissing, oohing and aahing could go on for a while, he thanked Egan and the nanny, and while they drove away, he got Laine moving back toward the house.

"I want to do more than just help with them," Tucker blurted out. "I want to be with them all the time. I want to feed them. Play with them." He paused. "Yeah, I'll even change 'em, often, but I'll let you know up front that's not something I especially want to do."

Though it no longer seemed like the chore it had been just a few days before. In fact, spending any kind of time with the pair would be something special.

"What exactly are you saying?" Laine asked.

Tucker fumbled around with this thought a moment and finally plucked out words that he hoped made sense. "I think we should make this legal and all. You should marry me and move into my house. Or your house. The location's irrelevant. Your answer, well, it isn't."

She stared at him as if he'd lost his mind, and for a few heart-stopping seconds, he thought he'd gotten this all wrong. That Laine's "I love you" hadn't meant the whole big dream that was now playing out in his head.

"Say yes," he prompted.

"Well, of course I'll say yes."

The relief caused him to make a funny breathing sound. Thank goodness it still managed to sound manly.

"Yes," she repeated.

Laine leaned in, kissed him. And that simple motion reminded him that once they had the babies put to bed, he wanted to strip off her clothes and make love to her again.

Plenty of times.

But first, he had to get something else off his chest.

"I'm in love with you, too, Laine."

The words felt darn good for something that'd never slipped past his tongue before. Tucker thought he'd be saying them for a long, long time.

Like the rest of their lives.

Laine pulled him to her and let him know that it was exactly what she had in mind, too.

* * * * *

USA TODAY *bestselling author Delores Fossen's new miniseries,* SWEETWATER RANCH, *continues next month. Look for* RUSTLING UP TROUBLE *wherever Harlequin Intrigue books are sold!*

COMING NEXT MONTH FROM

HARLEQUIN®

INTRIGUE®

Available October 21, 2014

#1527 RUSTLING UP TROUBLE
Sweetwater Ranch • by Delores Fossen
Deputy Rayanne McKinnon believes ATF agent Blue McCurdy, father to
her unborn child, is dead—until he shows up with hired killers on his trail
and no memory of their night together.

#1528 THE HUNK NEXT DOOR
The Specialists • by Debra Webb & Regan Black
Fearless Police Chief Abigail Jensen seized a drug shipment, halting
the cash flow of an embedded terrorist cell. Can undercover specialist
Riley O'Brien find the threat before the terrorists retaliate?

#1529 BONEYARD RIDGE
The Gates • by Paula Graves
To save her from a deadly ambush, undercover P.I. Hunter Bragg takes
Susannah Marsh on the run. But when their escape alerts a dangerous
enemy from Susannah's past, Hunter will need to rely on the other
members of The Gates to rescue the woman who healed his heart.

#1530 CROSSFIRE CHRISTMAS
The Precinct • by Julie Miller
When injured undercover cop Charlie Nash kidnapped nurse
Teresa Rodriguez to stitch up his wounds, he never meant to put his
brave rescuer in danger...or fall in love with her.

#1531 COLD CASE AT COBRA CREEK
by Rita Herron
Someone in town will do anything to stop Sage Freeport from getting the
truth about her missing son. Tracker Dugan Graystone's offer to help is
Sage's best chance to find her child...and lose her heart....

#1532 NIGHT OF THE RAVEN
by Jenna Ryan
When an old curse is recreated by someone seeking revenge, only
Ethan McVey, the mysterious new Raven's Cove police chief, stands
between Amara Bellam and a brutal killer.

HICNM1014

REQUEST YOUR FREE BOOKS!
2 FREE NOVELS PLUS 2 FREE GIFTS!

HARLEQUIN

INTRIGUE

BREATHTAKING ROMANTIC SUSPENSE

YES! Please send me 2 FREE Harlequin Intrigue® novels and my 2 FREE gifts (gifts are worth about $10). After receiving them, if I don't wish to receive any more books, I can return the shipping statement marked "cancel." If I don't cancel, I will receive 6 brand-new novels every month and be billed just $4.74 per book in the U.S. or $5.24 per book in Canada. That's a savings of at least 14% off the cover price! It's quite a bargain! Shipping and handling is just 50¢ per book in the U.S. and 75¢ per book in Canada.* I understand that accepting the 2 free books and gifts places me under no obligation to buy anything. I can always return a shipment and cancel at any time. Even if I never buy another book, the two free books and gifts are mine to keep forever.

182/382 HDN F42N

Name _____ (PLEASE PRINT) _____

Address _____ Apt. # _____

City _____ State/Prov. _____ Zip/Postal Code _____

Signature (if under 18, a parent or guardian must sign)

Mail to the **Harlequin® Reader Service:**
IN U.S.A.: P.O. Box 1867, Buffalo, NY 14240-1867
IN CANADA: P.O. Box 609, Fort Erie, Ontario L2A 5X3
**Are you a subscriber to Harlequin Intrigue books
and want to receive the larger-print edition?
Call 1-800-873-8635 or visit www.ReaderService.com.**

* Terms and prices subject to change without notice. Prices do not include applicable taxes. Sales tax applicable in N.Y. Canadian residents will be charged applicable taxes. Offer not valid in Quebec. This offer is limited to one order per household. Not valid for current subscribers to Harlequin Intrigue books. All orders subject to credit approval. Credit or debit balances in a customer's account(s) may be offset by any other outstanding balance owed by or to the customer. Please allow 4 to 6 weeks for delivery. Offer available while quantities last.

Your Privacy—The Harlequin® Reader Service is committed to protecting your privacy. Our Privacy Policy is available online at www.ReaderService.com or upon request from the Harlequin Reader Service.

We make a portion of our mailing list available to reputable third parties that offer products we believe may interest you. If you prefer that we not exchange your name with third parties, or if you wish to clarify or modify your communication preferences, please visit us at www.ReaderService.com/consumerschoice or write to us at Harlequin Reader Service Preference Service, P.O. Box 9062, Buffalo, NY 14269. Include your complete name and address.

HI13R

SPECIAL EXCERPT FROM

HARLEQUIN®

I N T R I G U E®

A surprise attack on her family ranch reunites a pregnant deputy with her baby's father—who supposedly died five months ago...

Read on for an excerpt from
RUSTLING UP TROUBLE
by USA TODAY bestselling author
Delores Fossen

She put her hand on his back to steady him. Bare skin on bare skin.

The hospital gown hardly qualified as a garment, with one side completely off his bandaged shoulder. Judging from the drafts he felt on various parts of his body, Rayanne was probably getting an eyeful.

Of course, it apparently wasn't something she hadn't already seen, since according to her they'd slept together five months ago.

"Will saying I'm sorry help?" he mumbled, and because he had no choice, he ditched the bargaining-position idea and lay back down.

"Nothing will help. As soon as you're back on your feet, I want you out of Sweetwater Springs and miles and miles away from McKinnon land. Got that?"

Oh, yeah. It was crystal clear.

It didn't matter that he didn't know why he'd done the things he had, but he'd screwed up. Maybe soon, Blue would remember everything that he might be trying to forget.

HIEXP69794

Her phone rang, the sound shooting through the room. And his head. Rayanne fished the phone from her pocket, looked at the screen and then moved to the other side of the room to take the call. It occurred to him then that she might be involved with someone.

Five months was a long time.

And this someone might be calling to make sure she was okay.

Blue felt the twinge of jealousy that throbbed right along with the pain in various parts of his body, and he wished he could just wake up from this crazy nightmare that he was having.

"No, he doesn't remember," she said to whoever had called. She turned to look back at him, but her coat shifted to the side.

Just enough for Blue to see the stomach bulge beneath her clothes.

Oh, man.

It felt as if someone had sucked the air right out of his lungs. He didn't need his memory to understand what that meant.

Rayanne was pregnant.

Find out how Rayanne reacts to Blue's discovery and what they plan to do to protect their unborn child when
RUSTLING UP TROUBLE
by USA TODAY bestselling author
Delores Fossen hits shelves in November 2014.